|||THE
|||CONTINUANCE

G.K. David II

Saberguette LLC.

Text copyright © 2022 By G.K. David II
ISBN-13: 978-0-578-26845-3

Published By Saberguette, LLC.
P.O. Box 205578
6102 5th Ave, Suite 1
Brooklyn, NY 11220
www.gkdavid.com

For Judge Jesus, Lala, Velita, Carmen, Courtney, and everyone else
that showed love when I did those football numbers on that
up north trip.

Fuck everyone who's racist. Change your ways or you all will share
Hell with the devil soon.

Introduction

At present writing, it is the year 2022. There are currently 9 different YouTube channels interviewing people that knew the immortal Tupac Shakur during his 25 years on earth.

The crazy thing is that he perished in 1996 (nearly 30 years ago), yet he is still the topic of many discussions as if he died a week ago.

This work of art that you are reading provides an alternative to a short-lived existence.

A tale is woven so brilliantly that this book had to be shortened. But no worries because part two is coming soon!

In the 2012 Quentin Tarantino blockbuster flick *DJANGO Unchained* (My fave flick of all time!), Jamie's character claims to be *"That 1 nigga in 10,000."*

Everyone can agree that 2pac could have said those words any day and the only reply he would have received was one word. FACTS!

To everyone that Almighty Jesus gave the opportunity to meet 'Pac during his time in this realm, I dedicate this to God and all of you lucky motherfuckas.

Preface

Hey readers, thanks for getting a copy of this book. I am a man that doesn't even read books unless that book is the Holy Bible so if you're just like me, but still plan on diving into this, then I must say that you won't be disappointed.

As I was writing this book, I received the same feeling that the men that wrote the Holy Bible must have felt.

I just KNEW that God was inspiring me and providing me with the ideas that were popping up in my thought process.

What I'm trying to say is, as I wrote this book I KNEW it was something that Almighty Jesus had Willed to happen.

So, that means that this book was written by GOD, not me. G.K. David II

Section 1

Four more shots

"I can't believe this bullshit!"

Tupac yelled in his mind as he woke up in a hospital bed in UMC of Southern Nevada. He tried to use his mouth to voice those words but for some reason, his mouth wouldn't work, nor could he muster up the strength to sit upright.

Suddenly all the memories of what happened 7 hours ago on the Vegas strip came flooding into his mind.

"Some motherfuckas shot me again?!'

He silently shouted in disbelief and shock, because it hadn't even reached two years since he first was struck by gunfire back in New York City in the fall of 1994.

A few seconds later his fiancée Kidada Jones entered the room with all the members of his *Outlaws* music group, as well as his close friend Treach from the hit-making rap group *Naughty By Nature*, and former Heavyweight boxing champ'-Mike Tyson-whose fight he attended the night before.

Kidada rushed over to his bed telling him she loved him as she kissed his forehead before he drifted back into a river of darkness losing consciousness due to comatose.

On the 6th day of the famed rapper's prolonged unconsciousness, he awakened again or so he thought. It was as if he was experiencing a dream because he was walking down a dirt road in a heavily wooded area, which he knew was impossible because he didn't feel any of the pain of a bullet-riddled body and collapsed lung as he did the first time he woke up.

"Yo, where the hell am I?" he questioned no one in particular, observing that he could finally hear his voice now, as he started walking down the narrow road, also noticing that he was wearing the same silk button-up shirt, denim jeans, and gold Gucci loafers that he wore at the MGM Casino on the night of his second shooting, which annoyed him because the dusty dirt from the road started coating them as he continued walking.

After several minutes Tupac heard breaking branches in the forest that lined the road and scenes from some of the old Friday the 13th movies started running through his mind, but instead of Jason Vorhees appearing from the brush with a machete in hand, a simple-looking Caucasian man walked towards him adorning white dress slacks and a plain white polo.

"Hello mate." He said with a slight English accent as he strode towards the cautious Shakur.

"Who the fuck are you?" Tupac replied getting ready for a fistfight if the stranger tried to attack him.

The slender-framed gent laughed and pleasantly urged him to be of good cheer because he was there to save his life and not harm him.

He then explained to the musical icon that he is an angel of the Lord, sent down to Earth to save his life-per God's Will, which will cause him to transform said life, inspiring millions of others to do so. This is one of the ways that the Lord brings humans into His Kingdom, basically taking them from a life of darkness and converting them into believers. Christians, as some call them.

"Maaaan, take yo' James Bond sounding ass back to London with that bullshit." Tupac laughed mockingly.

"If yo' ass got shot right now you would be leaking blood just like I did so how the fuck you an angel from Heaven?"

At that moment, the man supernaturally metamorphosized into Tupac's mother Afeni causing him to jump back in bewilderment.

"How the fuck did you do that?" he yelled at the angel that just turned into his mother before his very own eyes. The angel formally introduced himself as Nathaniel, still speaking in a British dialect while remaining in the form of Ms. Shakur which discomfited Tupac to the point of him yelling

"Stop this shit and change back to the white boy!" shaking the being's shoulders, demanding to know what was happening, until the angel shapeshifted back into the body that he appeared from the woodland.

At this point, Tupac calmed down and reasonably begged the angel-in-human-flesh to explain to him what was going on.

Nathaniel, then, spent the next few minutes re-explaining to him why God sent him down to earth.

Afterward, he magically made a black Holy Bible appear in his right hand and passed it to Tupac.

"Now allow me to show you previous times that the Lord has encountered other humans using angels that will help you understand your situation even better." He then instructed a visibly confused Tupac to turn the pages to the Book of Genesis, Chapter 18.

"Yo Nate I strongly believe that there's a God." Tupac interrupted. "I done wrote songs called Lord knows, Only God can judge me now, God bless the dead, Hail Mary, all that shit but I ain't never been through no shit like this before."

Nathaniel replied by quoting The Bible passage in the Book of James, chapter 2, verse 19, which reads: *Thou believest that there is one God; thou doest well: the devils also believe, and tremble.*

"Well Damn," Tupac interjected. "So, demons believe in God too but still go around doing evil shit? That don't make no sense."

Nate replied by mentioning Proverbs 16:4. *The Lord hath made all things for himself: yea, even the wicked for the day of evil.*

Nathaniel then asked him, a second time, to turn in the Bible he held, to the Book of Genesis, Chapter 18.

Tupac opened the thick, leather-covered book to the requested passage and started reading chapter 18, verses 20-33 at the urging of the smiling angel.

"And the Lord said, Because the cry of Sodom and Gomorrah is great, and because their sin is grievous.

I will go down now and see whether they have done altogether according to the cry of it, which is come unto me; and if not, I will know.

And the men turned their faces from thence and went toward Sodom: but Abraham stood yet before the Lord."

"Achoo!" Tupac sneezed before continuing.

"And Abraham drew near, and said, Wilt thou also destroy the righteous with the wicked?

Peradventure there be fifty righteous within the city: wilt thou also destroy and not spare the place for the fifty righteous that are therein?

That be far from thee to do after this manner, to slay the righteous with the wicked: and that the righteous should be as the wicked, that be far from thee: Shall not the Judge of all the earth do, right?

And the Lord said, If I find in Sodom fifty righteous within the city, then I will spare all the place for their sakes. And Abraham answered and said, Behold now, I have taken upon me to speak unto the Lord, which am but dust and ashes:

Peradventure there shall lack five of the fifty righteous: wilt thou destroy all the city for lack of five? And he said, If I find there forty and five, I will not destroy it.

And he spake unto him yet again, and said, Peradventure there shall be forty found there. And He said I will not do it for forty's sake.

And he said unto him, Oh let not the Lord be angry, and I will speak: Peradventure there shall thirty be found there. And he said I will not do it if I find thirty there.

And he said, Behold now, I have taken upon me to speak unto the Lord: Peradventure there shall be twenty found there. And he said I will not destroy it for twenty's sake.

And he said, Oh let not the Lord be angry, and I will speak yet but this once: Peradventure ten shall be found there. And he said I will not destroy it for ten's sake.

And the Lord went his way, as soon as he had left communing with Abraham: and Abraham returned unto his place."

Tupac looked at Nathaniel with interest and asked,

"So, Abraham was defending Sodom and Gomorrah by begging God not to bomb'em, which would kill the good people mixed in with the bad ones? That shit is crazy."

Sitting down, Indian style in the grass along the dirt road Nathaniel replied,

"Correct mate but start reading chapter 19 until I tell you to stop."

2pac glared at him for a second before continuing,

"And there came two angels to Sodom at even, and Lot sat in the gate of Sodom- hold up, hold up."

Tupac stopped reading.

"So those two angels were down here just like you are now?"

"Correct," Nathaniel answered. "They were in human bodies just as I am now but us angels are spirits by nature. There are several of us down here on Earth doing His Lordship's Work which is why He warned you, humans, to be careful of whom you come across down here because some of you have met us and didn't even realize that you were crossing paths with angels."

2pac smiled and blurted out

"Yo, that shit is deep!" before resuming.

"And Lot seeing them rose up to meet them, and he bowed himself with his face toward the ground.

And he said, Behold now, my lords, turn in, I pray you, into your servant's house, and tarry all night, and wash your feet, and ye shall rise early, and go on your ways. And they said, Nay; but we will abide in the street all night.

Section 1.2

"Okay, you can stop there," Nathaniel said.

"That was just one example of how His Lordship sends angels down to earth and places us in human bodies to do His work.

There are other passages in the Holy Bible showing how He did the same thing in different situations but I'm certain you are convinced that all of this is real, so I won't cover those scriptures with you."

"Hell, yea I believe this shit is real! I told you I got songs about God. I always felt a connection with the big man."

"Well, that's wonderful," Nathaniel said, unfolding his legs and rising from his position in the grass.

"Because now I am going to elaborate on the reason why Almighty God is saving your life from this second shooting, which surely would have killed you had He have not chosen to do so."

"Damn, so I was gonna die from this Vegas shit?" 2pac interjected while giving the angel man a bewildered look because surviving 5 bullet wounds in his first shooting gave him a sense of invincibility.

"Oh yes," Nathaniel replied. "In fact, you were scheduled to perish in the next hour and 17 minutes, if not for God's special plans for your life, which involves saving it, a second time, for a great purpose which we will go over now."

Before the angel-in-human-form finished speaking the landscape instantly changed from the gun-riddled rapper standing in the grassy area of the tree-lined dirt road to him sitting in the front row of a movie theater.

"What da fuck?" Tupac barked as he looked to his left and right in the lit cinema.

Then a familiar voice rang out causing him to sharply turn around. "You can always come back here with me if the front row is too close to the screen."

"Ay, man this David Copperfield shit you be doing is wild," 2pac uttered as he turned around to look at Nathaniel who was seated all the way in the center back row.

"You need to teach me how to do some of those magic tricks." He said jokingly as he got up from his position in front of the large room and made strides toward Nathaniel.

"Even If I wanted to do that it would be impossible mate," Nathaniel replied chuckling at the same time.

"You see If His Lordship gave you a portion of His Power you would only be able to use it to help someone else. It wouldn't work for you let's say if you wanted to vanish from here and instantly appear on South Beach, laying in the sand with a Daiquiri in your hand."

"Well, why not?" Shakur asked inquisitively as he sat down in the stiff-cushioned seat next to the angel.

"Because The Lord's power is governed by a law that won't permit it to be abused for selfish reasons."

This explanation went into one ear and out of the other because 2pac gave Nathaniel a look of puzzlement.

"That don't even make sense!" he said matter-of-factly.

"We was just in the woods somewhere, and in the blink of an eye we popped up in this movie theater. You just used God's power to do that, but I don't see you helping me with shit."

Nathaniel grinned and replied, "Actually I am helping you, which leads to the next phase of this continuance objective that God has for you."

The angel motioned with his head for Tupac to look ahead at the big screen as the lights suddenly dimmed on cue.

"I am about to show you why God saved your life again and what you'll be doing with your remaining time on earth. Now, pay close attention to all the information and instructions I give you."

2pac glared at the silver screen as he watched himself riding in a black BMW with his record label's boss as they came upon a red light. Moments later he watched himself being struck by multiple rounds as a white Cadillac sedan pulled up alongside the sleek, luxury car, and a rear passenger fired shots at him seconds later.

"That bitch ass nigga from the casino got me?

" 2pac yelled out as he realized that the drive-by was a retaliation move due to an incident earlier that night when he led an attack on a man that reportedly stole a necklace from one of his record label's associates.

"I don't want to do this to you, but you force my hand Tupac!"

Nathaniel cried out. "I understand that you are outspoken and you're a say what's on your mind kind of bloke, but you must not interrupt again. Everything that is happening right now is because of Almighty God, therefore this stuff is of the utmost importance.

Because I don't believe you will be able to contain yourself I, hereby, use the power vested in me, by The Lord God, to close your vocal cords, disallowing you to speak again until I open them back up."

"Man, chill out! I was just realizing who it was that shot me." 2pac yelled fiercely instantly perceiving that the words that he just formed didn't flow out of his mouth like he expected them to.

Section 1.5

"Damn, this mothafucka took my voice for real." The defeated rapper said to himself as he looked at the angel man serenely to let him know that he accepts his defeat.

Pleased with 2pac's instantly changed attitude the servant of the Lord continued where he left off.

"Now, as I was saying, I am about to explain to you why God saved your life again and what you'll be doing with your remaining time on earth. He said motioning for Tupac to look back ahead at the movie screen as scenes of him lying in a hospital bed flashed before his eyes.

Shakur watched, fascinated, as millions of fans mourned him after his mother decided to have the medical staff pull the plug on his life support machinery, and how his music was still being released years after he passed away.

It felt like he was watching a sci-fi flick as the movie of what was his life continued and he saw how technology advanced from 1996 onward.

"What is an iPhone?"

He asked as he saw fans using them to listen to his final album, released in 2006.

"Oh, shit they made a movie about me?!" He rose from his seat intrigued that the actor they used to play him in the 2017 film looked exactly like him and even had the same mannerism and a similar voice as his.

"That shit didn't go down like that." 2pac noticed that one of the scenes from the movie was untruthfully depicted before the screen started dimming and the theater lights came back on, temporarily blinding him. He glared at Nathaniel, annoyed that the movie was stopped in the middle of his enjoyment.

"Okay, so you see how your life is going to turn out after you die." Nathaniel shifted in his seat.

"But His Lordship is about to change all of that by bringing you out of the coma you are currently in and giving you a mission in your new lease on life."

"Man, I ain't no damn Christian!" 2Pac barked out, in his mind, as he recoiled in distaste at the thought of quitting smoking marijuana and cigarettes, and never tasting the smooth bitterness of a mouthful of Hennessy cognac again.

The angel man erupted in laughter because he had the ability to read the rapper's thoughts and heard what he said.

"Not everyone that serves God is a Christian Tupac," Nathaniel said matter-of-factly as he opened the same Holy Bible that 2Pac had read from on the dirt road.

"In the Book of Proverbs, Chapter 16, verse 4 it says that *The Lord has made all things for Himself, even the wicked for the day of evil.*"

"So, all the wicked people, or wicked things that God has created for Himself is serving His purpose just like you will be doing, despite not having the reputation of someone who is a man of God. You understand?"

2Pac nodded his bald head in agreement, realizing that the Holy Bible is a more interesting Book than he thought it was.

"From this moment forward the Lord wants you to change your image and live your life more positively so you can become a good influence on others whose lives will turn out for the worse if you remain the same thug rapper that you are known for now."

This caused a stir and a scowl because the iconic rapper enjoyed his current level of success, save for the situation with him desiring to leave his record label to form his own company.

"And after you go forward and start motivating others to do right, through your changed actions, God has one final mission for you, which is to assist a future music artist in his transition from near-death to continuance. This will take place in a human decade or so, which gives you a very extended stay down here on this present planet Earth.

"When that time arrives, He will grant you the same powers He has entrusted me with to complete that final mission, as well as supernaturally downloading all of the instructions into your memory bank so you will know exactly what to do."

All this information that he was taking in caused Shakur to just lean back in his rigid seat as if having just inhaled an exotic strain of marijuana that was causing him to have hallucinations and consciousness expansion.

"This shit is outta this world." 'Pac uttered, feeling a tingling in his ears as he realized that he could hear his voice again.

"Well, thanks for giving me my shit back, and I don't mean no harm when I be saying stuff, I'm just a man that speaks my mind and speaks the truth about shit no matter who it's to."

"Yes," The angel agreed nodding his head.

"This is the reason His Lordship has chosen you for this big mission."

And in the blink of the rapper's glistening eyes, the angel of the Lord vanished into thin air.

"Yo, where you go, Nathaniel?" Tupac shouted out in the humongous room, looking all around before noticing that he was getting extremely sleepy. He then laid down on the cold theater floor, in between the rows of seats and drifted off into a heavy sleep.

Section 2:

Miracle Man

After what felt like days had gone by muffled voices started surfacing in his auditory range, causing him to attempt to gain consciousness because he realized that he was slightly shivering and remembered that he had fallen asleep on a cold, movie theater floor.

2Pac struggled to lift himself up as the voices near him became clearer.

He was astonished to see two nurses handling equipment around him as he slowly opened his eyes and noticed that his body was in excruciating pain as he lay in an air-conditioned hospital room.

Then, a group of doctors and other medical personnel rushed into the room all wearing stunned facial expressions, puzzled at the fact that their patient was awake, and pulling at the restraints holding his wrists to the bed rails, despite having enough Pentobarbital in his body to keep an elephant asleep for days.

"Ayyy why'm cffddd?" Tupac asked making gargling and burbling sounds as the ventilator tubes going into his mouth impeded clear speech.

"Don't try to talk Mr. Shakur."

A tall middle-aged doctor named Ron Fildes said as he started pressing buttons on the life support machine.

"We had to strap you down a few days ago when you kept trying to get out of bed. We apologize for the inconvenience and will have them removed soon."

"This is unbelievable!"

another doctor chimed in because the patient's mother was just discussing with the group her intention of having her son taken off of the support machinery so his soul would have an uninterrupted passage into the afterlife.

2Pac's eyes were wide open as he tossed his head around looking at all the commotion going on around him as two of the other men in the group began untying the leather wrist restraints, freeing the rapper's hands.

2Pac motioned for one of them to give him a cigarette, making a hand gesture as if he was smoking, causing them both to shake their heads from left to right.

"Mr. Shakur, you only have one lung in your body now so the last thing you need is a cancer stick." Dr. Fildes spoke up as he began writing numbers down in a notepad that was tucked in his lab coat's front pocket.

After another half hour of fiddling around with the equipment in the room, everyone started streaming out as his mother rushed in excited to see her son's eyes open and alert.

"Boy, do you know I was about to -- "Afeni fussed before stopping herself, realizing she was about to tell her son that she was going to have doctors pull the plugs on the life support system that was keeping him breathing.

Instead of continuing communication with her mouth, she instead grabbed a nearby notepad and pen and spent the rest of that afternoon talking with her son on paper.

Section 2.2

The healing rapper spent the next 47 days in the Las Vegas medical center before being moved to a rehabilitation facility in San Diego where he spent another 8 weeks resting and healing from all the trauma to his 156-pound frame.

Within that time, it seemed like every media outlet in the world did an article on the immortal rapper's second brush with death and how many units his next album was projected to sell, due to his legend increasing tenfold after pulling through a second shooting

Because of this seeming immortality that he appeared to possess, Suge Knight, the owner of his record label and close friend increased pressure on him to release another album immediately despite a lack of willingness from the still healing man whose breathing was heavier now that he was only operating with one lung.

What 2Pac didn't know yet was that Knight's attorney had recently informed the bearish man that he may possibly be looking at prison time due to his involvement in the attack on the gangbanger at the MGM Grand before the drive-by occurred.

The music mogul's probation officer caught wind of his famous client's involvement in the beating, primarily because it was captured on the casino's state-of-the-art camera surveillance system.

The veteran lawyer was doing everything he could to keep the ex-football player from going behind bars but the video of him kicking the helpless victim while he was on the ground was damning.

During the last few months leading up to Suge's court date, 2Pac began accepting interviews from most of the masses of news outlets that had been hounding his publicists after his release from the hospital, for Q-and-A sessions, most of them offering hefty amounts of money for the chance to talk with the rapper who made a song about taking 5 shots and smiling while doing so.

His main theme, in each of these sit-down sessions, was that his feud with the fellow rapper- The Notorious B.I.G.- was over and he is a changed man now after surviving death once again.

He also emphasized that he is on a mission from God to make positive changes in the world of rap, which befuddled his millions of fans who were used to his in-your-face attitude and the thug life persona that he'd been displaying for the last 3 ½ years.

With time winding down to his potential incarceration at his upcoming court date, a conniving Suge Knight arranged for a group of his henchmen to pop up at Tupac's residence and threaten him into going into the studio to begin recording songs for a new LP, a method that the wicked boss had used against other rappers in previous occasions, but the ploy didn't work this time because of the fiery heart that the bullet-scarred artist still possessed despite his encounter with Holiness.

After pulling out an unregistered handgun that he had obtained years ago 2Pac aimed at the four men and promised to shoot them all if they didn't retreat from his doorstep, which they all did because if they called his bluff and ended up murdering him, he would never be able to make another album as a living being, which will generate more millions for their bosses' pockets.

When Knight got the news while sitting in his spacious office, he got so angry that he picked up his cigar humidor and threw it at the large windows, hitting one and causing a huge spider web of a crack.

Before the bitter CEO could threaten Shakur again, he was sentenced to 9 years in prison for probation violation, and there began the fall of his ownership of his world-famous music label.

When 2Pac heard about his latest foe's sentencing and incarceration you would have expected him to go out and celebrate not having that pressure in his life anymore, but he actually felt the opposite way.

The same cameras that captured Suge's vicious kick also captured the fearless rapper leading the charge and striking the first blow, which started the whole melee, and just as his suspicion had kept him up every night since Knight's jailing, three weeks later he received the dreaded phone call that he had to return to New York City for his own court date.

In spite of hiring 2 of New York's best defense attorneys to represent him, the once gangsta rapper had his appeal bond revoked by the New York appellate courts and was shipped back to the same cruddy correctional facility that he spent most of 1995 in.

Only having another 3 years left on his original sentence should have comforted the depressed emcee but it didn't.

After experiencing several moments of opulence as one of his record label's top artists less than a year ago, and now reduced to property of the state of New York-AGAIN- made those upcoming 3 years feel like he had to serve 3 centuries.

Forced to serve his time in protective custody due to his celebrity status and the potential threats on his life out in the prison's general population, 2Pac found himself cursing out God the first night into his re-imprisonment, as he sat on the edge of the rigid prison mattress in his damp cell, looking upward at the ceiling as if he was actually laying eyes on Jesus Christ sitting in Heaven on His Throne.

"Man fuck you, God!"

The disgruntled inmate snarled in the direction of the ceiling.

"I wasn't gonna do no more thug music, and I was gonna do everything you wanted me to do but now I'm saying fuck you God since you wanna put me back in this bullshit!"

Section 3:

A special conception

A sweaty man pumped hard for several minutes until he climaxed into his wife's sweet-smelling, clammy cavity, causing 97 million spermatozoa bullets to be shot inside of her.

Several of those cells began forming a gel around them to provide protection from the acidic territory of her vagina while racing through her body, entering her uterus and forward to her fallopian tubes.

By this time there were only 29 million sperm cells left to compete for contact with one of the woman's eggs.

Under the supernatural control of Almighty God, one particular sperm, which would later be named Jarad, had its speed boosted which allowed it to reach an egg mere seconds before one of its competitors was able to do so.

9 months later, the human whom 'Pac was designated to encounter in the future, was born in a Chicago hospital to proud parents, one of whom would leave the household during the baby's third year on earth.

Section 3.3:

A special visit

2Pac broke down and started crying profusely because, what he didn't know was that, during his encounter with the angel named Nathaniel Almighty God had implanted His Holy Spirit inside of his tattooed body, so now God dwelled in him although he didn't appear to be a born-again Christian yet.

In view of this fact, when the re-incarcerated rapper began cursing the Lord, it caused a war between his human spirit and the Holy Spirit, both of whom were now sharing his body.

Shakur continued swearing and blaming God for the events that led to the depression that was starting to overwhelm him in his claustrophobic holding place and cause him to get on his knees as he covered his dampened face in the crease of his arms, the tears ceasing to stop falling.

"It's gonna be alright brother Shakur." A voice that mostly everyone has heard, at some point, in their lifetime circulated throughout the tiny, 6' X 8' cell.

"What da fuck!" Tupac blurted out, surprisingly. "I know Martin mothafuckin' Luther King ain't in my cell right now?"

He finished his sentence with exhilarated disbelief, shocked that the man who did so much for his race of people was actually right before his eyes in human flesh looking exactly as he did back in 1968 before his assassination.

To show his reverence for the slain, civil rights leader, 2Pac immediately started addressing him as sir.

"Umm, sir, I understand that this is something that God is doing but these prison walls are thin as fuck, excuse my French, and people can hear you."

The resurrected Baptist minister smiled and explained that no one can hear them even though some inmates were still awake in neighboring cells because the Lord has deafened their ears to the words being spoken by both men during the supernatural visit.

"This shit just keeps gettin' crazier and crazier" 'Pac expressed using his prison-issued tank top to wipe the moisture from his face.

Dr. King then motioned for him to sit down next to him on the prison cot as he passed along instructions from the Lord, in his slow southern drawl, revealing that God placed the rapper back in prison for a specific reason and reminded him that the same God also sent him- a Baptist preacher-to jail 29 times, back in the 1950s and '60s for civil rights-related incidents.

God's intentions are to ground him in His Word-The Holy Bible-without any distractions, by having him read the entire book from cover to cover, and what better place to do that than the Clinton correctional facility's special housing unit.

The world-renown pastor sat with 2Pac for another hour, elaborating on the instructions that he passed along from Heaven, and sharing a few of his own experiences with the Lord, all of which accelerated the rapper's current depression recovery, and as magically as the minister appeared he was gone but he made his mark and the multi-platinum selling rapper went to sleep with a smile on his face that night, confident in what he had to accomplish.

In the following weeks, Tupac obtained a Bible from the prison chapel and began reading it from the beginning. Although the "gangsta" rapper made several references to God in his music, he had never actually read God's Word, so as he got deeper into the Book, he started noticing how cool the stories in it were.

The accounts of Eve, the first woman on earth, being encountered by a talking snake, and God making a huge sea eerily split in half so His people could escape a storming army fascinated him and increased his desire to read more.

Section 4:

The gambler

During this time, up in the Heavenly Dimension, angels held a conference with Almighty God reporting on the results of their duties and recent missions when Satan popped in to join the group.

"What in Hell do you want?"

The angel Nathaniel uttered in distaste as he stared at the conniver.

Ignoring him, Satan cut right to the chase by going over to The Lord and asking permission to speak, which was granted by Jah immediately.

"Hey, how ya doing Lord-Uhm I meant former Lord?"

Satan asked with a smirk.

God looked at his archenemy, shaking His head in a Tsk-Tsking gesture.

"You see that we are having a meeting so say what you have to say and then get out."

"Yes, yes." The leader of the devils replied.

"I'm here to inquire about the human named Tupac Shakur. I want to know what you're doing down there with him and why you're trying to change him from the popular thug from the Westside to one of your- what's the name they use down there to describe your minions?

"They call themselves Christians you nitwit and what's it to you?

An angel named Bartholomew chimed in.

Ignoring him as well, as he does all his former counterparts due to believing they're beneath him, Satan continued his dialogue with the Deity in front of him.

"Yes, that's the term. Christian. Why are you trying to change Tupac into a Christian?

"I knew the 'Pac Plan" would bother you." The Lord replied laughing.

"I allowed you to control Tupac's life for these past 25 human years and you influenced him to live a gangster lifestyle getting high and drinking that intoxicant called Hennessy every day, as well as a host of other sinful things but it was all a part of my plan and now, he's about to do a 360 and shock the human world."

"That sounds stupid!" Satan barked back in a disdainful tone causing several nearby angels to rise up in alertness as if they were about to throw a pesky patron out of a bar.

"I'll bet you that if you let me reach out and touch him that I'll get him to remain the thug that he will always be."

There was a sudden silence in the large room followed by The Lord finally responding in agreeance but warning Satan not to lay one finger on Tupac's person.

What the devil didn't know was this consensus was actually part of God's Plan, just as it was a gazillion human years ago when He allowed Satan to do similar tests on His servant Job.

Satan exited the meeting area with a cheerful stride, comforted that he wasn't going to lose control of the influential human named

Tupac, who was a musician just as he had been before being kicked out of his residence in The Kingdom of Heaven.

Section 5

While the devil was wheeling and dealing up in Heaven, 2Pac was laying in his solemn cell meditating when he came up with the idea to launch a nonprofit organization upon his release from prison which he would name: T.H.U.G. Life Ministries. The acronym 'T.H.U.G.' stood for the words, truly holy unto God, and he would use the platform to give out Holy Bibles and free food to poor people around the world.

He spent the next few days jotting down ideas and reading his Bible when a new face appeared in his cell's window as the tray flap, in the middle of the metal door, was opened.

A large, jet-black man ordered 2Pac to come and place his hands through the rectangular opening so he could secure handcuffs on him and escort him to see an unknown visitor.

Every inmate that was in solitary confinement had to be handcuffed before leaving their cell and 2Pac hated it because the cuffs increased his claustrophobia.

"Never seen you here before. You a new C.O.?" 2Pac shuffled down a damp corridor next to the 6'4" giant man, attempting to make small talk.

The quiet correctional officer glared down at the popular inmate with a menacing look before reaching out and slapping him with enough force to knock the state-issued spectacles that Tupac began wearing, 20 yards down the hallway.

"What da fuck you do that for C.O.?" The enraged rapper yelled out, causing Officer Brown to look around and make sure no one saw the attack.

"You little piece of shit, you better hope I don't finally kill yo' ass for what you did!" Brown replied in a low angry tone.

He then snatched Tupac, who provided no resistance due to being handcuffed from behind, and pushed him into a dark mop closet.

"Nigga I ain't never seen you in my life!"

He protested as he contemplated kicking the larger man in his groin.

"You got my cousin killed motherfucka!" Brown barked back.

"Christopher was my 2nd cousin, and he wouldn't've gotten killed if it wasn't for yo' bitch ass. We was 'bout to start a label and everything!"

With this current information, a quick-thinking 'Pac realized what was happening and shared the fact that he apologized to Biggie before he was murdered, as well as all of the other artists that he had been feuding with the previous year, but the seething C.O. quickly replied,

"Yeah, nigga but that fuckin' song you made got into those west coast niggas' minds and caused them to do that shit!"

Brown said referencing 2Pac's huge diss record about B.I.G. called *Hit'em up* which flew to the top of the charts last year.

"I understand that you mad."

'Pac started saying as he recalled a Bible verse, he had read earlier about The Lord making peoples' enemies their footstools, which caused him to silently pray for help as the burly man grabbed his neck and started applying pressure.

A helpless, bulging-eyed Shakur continued to pray in his head not sure if God would save him or he would finally get murdered when the door was yanked open and several of Brown's fellow officers rushed in and tackled the 300 pounder as if auditioning at the NFL combine.

It took 6 of the 9 guards there to restrain Brown and as he was led away in handcuffs The Holy Spirit whispered in the heavily breathing actor

"Satan just tried to take you away, but God will always save you when you call on Him."

Which comforted him as he was slowly led to the infirmary for medical attention.

God continued testing Tupac in the ensuing months, none of them as hard as that first trial, and the rapper easily passed most of them, so The Lord decided to bless him with an early release, just as he wrapped up the last few chapters in the Book of Revelation.

2pac was excited when he received the good news and gave away all his commissary, and other items he had accumulated in the dreary upstate New York hellhole.

"Mama!" A freed Shakur yelled gleefully as he ran through the open gates as two armed guards watched.

Tupac hugged his mother before they hopped in the back of a chauffeured Suburban.

His mother managed his finances during his incarceration and even hired an attorney for him who filed a lawsuit against the new owners of his former record label for royalties that were still owed him.

That was an easy victory, and the rapper added a cool 5 million dollars to his once-empty bank account.

As for his fiancée, Kidada Jones, she loved the reformed rapper and he loved her as well, but they decided to call off their engagement while he was still imprisoned after she confessed that his life makeover is the reason for her lack of wanting to remain committed.

This logic confused a talkative Tupac and he wrote letter after letter to her demanding that she break down exactly what in the hell she meant by that until she finally elaborated by telling him that she fell in love with Tupac the Thug and wanted to marry him because SHE was influencing him to eat better, do better, so he would become better, but now that he's on some spiritual trip and God has taken over her job, it caused her to lose that desire to be his wife, although she pledged to be his best friend forever, and now maintains the same level of friendship with him as his other female friend Jada Pinkett-Smith does.

Section 6:

Puttin' in Ministry work

Over the next couple of years, the ci-devant thug spent his time operating T.H.U.G. Life ministries and rejecting offers from various rappers to do features on their projects.

Most of the artists had gangster images and wanted the 'old' 'Pac back but The Lord had him grounded enough not to fall into temptation and return to a studio to record music about killing people and degrading women.

In the background of Tupac's new lease on life, Satan continued machinating against his adversary, Almighty God, by attempting to ensnare 2Pac in traps but nothing was working until he decided to send a woman his way that he could easily use to get him caught up into something that would piss God off and so he arranged for the T.H.U.G. Life Ministries founder to sit next to a beautiful, Brooklyn goddess by the name of Inga Marchand, on a flight from LAX to La Guardia.

"Oh, shit they got me sitting next to 'Pac."

The newest woman to rise in the world of rap music said excitedly as she lowered her fantastic fanny down into the seat next to his.

"Oh snap, Fox Boogie in the house!"

Tupac looked at her smiling as he closed a magazine he had been thumbing through.

This wasn't their first encounter. The two had first met when her manager and she met up with 2pac about doing a song with her on her debut album, which he declined.

Despite the rejection, she didn't hold a grudge against the healing rapper and loved his vibe.

They reminisced about that initial contact before discussing their destinations.

2pac was headed to New York to meet with a company interested in sponsoring his nonprofit organization, and Foxy was returning home from a Hawaii photo shoot that her label was going to use for the promotion of her upcoming sophomore LP.

After mentioning the soon release of that second album Satan entered her mind and began to negatively influence her which led her to feign distress over him turning her down that first time and expressing how much she wanted to do a song with the rapper, which had been a dream of hers since hearing his chart-topping song from 1993 titled "Keep ya head up".

A focused Tupac did his best to emphasize that he was sorry but he still couldn't do a song with his gorgeous acquaintance when she thrust her manicured hand under the bulky Pelle Pelle coat that blanketed his lap, and that hand's mission was to breach the zippered slot in his baggy *Girbaud* jeans, by unfastening them and slipping under his boxer's garment, grabbing ahold of his manhood and stroking it as if letting it go would cause the plane to crash.

An uneasy 2pac squirmed in his seat and looked around for neighbors but they nearly had first-class to themselves on this flight.

Letting his guard down, the sex-starved spiritualist remote-controlled a hand of his own to duck up under the tight skirt that Foxy adorned and find its way to her steamy cave of satisfaction.

As his once nicotine-stained fingers popped in and out of her, the young rapper began gyrating against the half-comfy airplane seat cushion as 'Pac's fingers kept popping to a tune of their own.

Not being able to contain herself, Inga tried to stifle a scream but only accomplished half of it.

A nearby napping flight attendant received the other half and immediately jumped into investigation mode zeroing in on the musicians as they made weak attempts to make things look normal.

"Look here guys, this ain't no damn mile high club so if you don't want to get separated, I suggest you knock it off."

A stone-faced, redhead of about 55 years barked at Foxy and 'Pac as they laughed at her, agreeing to behave themselves.

Shakur started battling instant thoughts of regret because having sex without being married to a woman is fornication according to the Bible but the newly formed lust for this chocolate goddess was starting to overwhelm him.

The Holy Bible's Book of Romans, Chapter 3, verse 23 says that every human being was born a sinner.

When God chose that He would make someone a believer in Him, He selects a day in their life when He places His Holy Spirit inside of their body, and from that day forward, The Holy Spirit does His job of comforting and convicting someone when they decide to commit further sin.

Most people call this having a guilty conscience, and Tupac totally ignored his guilt while making plans to have dinner with Foxy Brown at her Westchester County mansion that upcoming weekend.

On the night of that dinner date, an excited Tupac hopped in the back of the stretch Ford Expedition Limousine that the lady of the night sent down to his Manhattan hotel to retrieve him, not even waiting for the driver to courteously open his door for him.

As the thrilled gospel gangsta helped himself to some of the champagne in the extended truck's mini-bar he noticed something laying on the extensive seat to his left.

He peeled off the stick it note stuck to the crotch portion of the Saint Laurent, lace thong laying on the seat beside him, and felt his eyes enlarge as he read the words,

'Smell your dinner.' Which was written on the small, yellow piece of paper.

"This girl is freaky!"

Tupac grinned to himself, deeply inhaling the agreeable scent of the red panties that he clutched in his right hand, as the limousine made its way up Interstate 87 North towards the night's pleasure.

Upon arrival at Inga's 3-million-dollar Ardsley, NY home a relaxed Tupac complimented her on her success and made sure to let her know that he enjoyed the surprise that he found in the limo which drew a laugh out of the immaculately dressed artist who adorned a sexy, Christian Dior skirt that highlighted her luscious legs.

After a delicious dinner prepared by her part-time chef, she enticed 2pac to join her in her custom-built, home studio, where the slightly inebriated rapper was seduced into recording the long-awaited song that she had been yearning for, for the past three years.

It only took him half an hour to pen the 16-bar verse while Foxy, a far cry from a recording engineer, learned enough to be capable of recording 'Pac's verse, so the real engineer would be able to add it to her song.

Gratified that one of rap's most highly sought after artists, and a man that she highly admired was going to be on her next album, a fearless Foxy began disrobing as Tupac exited the tiny studio booth, hopping into his arms wearing nothing but the layers of smooth skin that God gave her, prompting him to follow suit, laying her naked-ness down on the carpeted studio floor and thrusting his tongue so far up inside of her that his saliva on the inner parts of her labia.

The pair enjoyed sexual acts the rest of that night and Tupac de-cided to extend his trip, caught in the grasp of the beautiful rapper.

2pac's verse on Foxy's second album was the first time he had made any kind of music after the Vegas shooting so this helped her sell over 7 million copies and solidify her as a force to be reckoned with in the world of hip hop.

The couple continued seeing each other although they never con-firmed that they were dating.

Section 6:

2pac Back!?!?

The media began attacking the supposedly reformed rapper with magazine headlines like

'So, is the real 2pac back?'

And other articles along those lines, which began tarnishing his transformed image.

He began neglecting the daily duties of operating his nonprofit in favor of running around with Foxy, as Satan's grip on her gave rise to him smoking weed again, despite a burning chest from only having one lung, and reuniting with his favorite beverage. Hennessy cognac.

"It looks like the old 2pac is back." Satan giggle-talked as he waltzed in the room during the middle of one of Almighty God's Heavenly conferences a few weeks later.

All the angels in attendance glared at the jokester murderously as God the Father spoke.

"It appears as if that is true, but it is not. Everything happens for a reason Satan. My reasons!"

Yahweh finished before snapping His fingers, causing a smug Satan to suddenly vanish into thin air.

By this time, 2pac had basically taken up residence in the state of New York to be closer to his quasi-mega star girlfriend, Foxy Brown, despite her spending less time with him due to the hectic schedule she maintained after selling so many records a few months earlier.

Section 6.6:

Disappointment leads to destiny

One night after exhausting love-making due to not seeing each other for the past fifty days Foxy made plans with 'Pac to attend the grand opening of her friend Jay-Z's- 40/40 club.

Tupac, once an adversary of the famous rapper immediately agreed because after the Vegas shooting he apologized to everyone that he had ever disrespected and that apols moved everyone to forgive him.

On the night of the outing, Inga and Tupac agreed to arrive separately, despite having feelings for each other, because they weren't ready to announce to the world that they were an item, which allowed a plan that her ex-fiancé, Kurupt, a fellow rapper, to implement with ease.

The rapper Kurupt ironically was once one of 2pac's label mates.

He got engaged to Foxy Brown in 1997, but they postponed this engagement just a few months before fate aligned her with 2pac on that flight from L.A. to N.Y.

Kurupt never really got over his feelings for the beautiful, Brooklyn queen, therefore he plotted ways to win her heart back.

When he heard she would be attending Jay-Z's club opening event he didn't hesitate to formulate a stratagem to re-enter her life.

Upon her arrival at the occasion, Foxy was stupefied by the horse-drawn carriage that Kurupt motioned her to come to join him in as she got out of her limo in front of the venue.

The Philly-born, West coaster had never displayed this level of romanticism since she had known him, so the platinum-selling princess was blown away and all of her past feelings for him came rushing back.

Needless to say, Foxy never made it to the function that night and a deserted Tupac had to control his disappointment as he made his rounds around the posh sports bar, running into a woman that would ultimately become his wife one day.

"Well, is it true what you said in your song about age ain't nothing but a number?" Tupac asked a beautiful young woman as she strode past him.

Surprised that the man who survived two shootings spoke to her, Aaliyah stopped in front of him just looking wide-eyed not knowing what to say, her introvert personality kicking in.

"It's true in my world."

She finally replied as 'Pac continued the conversation in an attempt to repair his bruised ego thanks to Foxy's sudden abandonment.

The sultry singer stood there absorbing his wordplay before mentioning that most of the music industry suspects that he is dating rapper Foxy Brown which he admitted so until she weirdly dumped him tonight thanks to rekindlement efforts by her ex-fiancé, which caused Aaliyah to feel sympathy for 'Pac due to everything he went through with his shootings and reformation.

They spent another hour chatting before the slick-talking poet asked her for her phone number which Aaliyah politely refused.

2pac returned to California the following morning but started thinking about his encounter with Aaliyah every day until fantasies of being with her started forming in his mind.

Section 7

There was no such thing as social media in these days, so an anxious Shakur started sharing his dilemma with a few of his acquaintances who were connected to the music industry.

Ronnie, a bodyguard shaped like Bruce Banner when his skin color changed to green, mentioned that his cousin, also a bodyguard, recently landed a gig working security for 2pac's ex-fiancée Kidada Jones, and how he was elated to meet her best friend, Aaliyah, whom he is a huge fan of and was in attendance with Kidada at some Tommy Hilfiger fashion show a few weeks ago in Manhattan.

A stunned Tupac couldn't believe the words that had just come out of his friend Ronnie's mouth and reverted to the gutter language of his thug days to question him.

"Nigga are you saying that Kidada and Aaliyah are best friends?"

2pac got his answer when Ronnie uttered the word

"Duhhhh."

And immediately grabbed his Motorola 2-way pager to contact his former, future wife, Kidada.

Quincy Jones' daughter was the first woman that the street-raised rapper fell in love with so she would always have a place in his heart, so when he finally got in contact with her, after several attempts due to her busy itinerary, he proceeded with caution, so as not to disrespect her in any way.

Kidada would always have a space in her heart for Tupac as well, but the phone calls decreased during his classified courtship of Foxy Brown, therefore they hadn't spoken for half a year before he reached out to her at this time.

"Hey mean man, how've you been doing?"

Kidada asked jokingly, referring to a pet name she used to call Shakur when they were engaged because his attitude would always change for the worse when he ingested too much Hennessy cognac.

A humble 2pac laughed then commenced to exchange pleasantries and catch up with everything that happened to his friend in the past 6 months.

After an hour of chit-chat, 2pac felt that his beautiful friend was comfortable enough with him to answer his next question without enviousness, so he explained how he met Aaliyah a few months ago in New York and developed an intense crush on her.

Before he could finish talking Kidada abruptly interposed him by disclosing a revelation that suddenly increased his faith in Jesus Christ.

His erstwhile prospective spouse revealed that her bestie also has a crush on him because she talks about him constantly and has even started listening to his music.

Something she never did before, so Kidada suspected that something was going on and expressed to 'Pac that there have been others that have requested she hook them up with her precious gal pal, but she always refused because of the lifestyles these men were living.

Kidada tearfully promised to pass his number to Aaliyah because she felt deep down in her heart that this is what the higher power she called *The Universe* wanted her to do.

From the moment Tupac received the first call from Aaliyah there wasn't a day that passed that he didn't call her, and it was these conversations that effectuated her decision not to move forward in her friendship with Dame Dash, a well-known music executive with whom she'd recently gotten close to and pondered dating.

Regardless of a near decade-long age gap, the 22-year-old Aaliyah was head over heels in love with 2pac after a mere month of diurnal heart-to-hearts.

They both agreed to announce that they were an item at her 3rd album's release party that July and the media world went into a frenzy releasing article after article about the pair.

The following month Shakur made the decision to leave his beloved state of California and return to his origins so he could be closer to the woman that he felt he was more in love with than he was with her BFF back in 1996.

Aaliyah resided in the Parker-Meridien Hotel, as she was having a house built from scratch out in the Hamptons, so Tupac secured a rental unit in Zero World Trade Center, the third monstrous skyscraper that made up the triplet twin towers that opened back in 1973.

The one-time New Yorker felt like he was being robbed when he moved into his 87th floor flat in the 110-floor tower but he thoughtfully ignored the absurdity of paying $5600 a month for 2 bedrooms because of the comforting fantasies that ran through his mind of living in a Hamptons mansion with his future wife in less than a year.

Section 7:

New York must die!!!

The alarm clock blared loudly like a speeding cop car as Aaliyah awakened, punching the button to make the noise cease. The homebody had an 11 a.m. session at the same recording studio where her boyfriend experienced five gunshots to his slender frame, almost 7 years ago so she hopped out of bed and jumped into her shower to begin her morning.

As she scrubbed her athletic body with a soapy hand cloth, she noticed her Nokia 8250 vibrating on the sink counter and stepped out of the steamy bliss to answer the call.

On the other end, her brother Rashad was screaming at the top of his lungs about World War 3 and how she had to get out of New York City immediately.

After calming him down and getting a clearer explanation of what had him so worked up, she quickly turned on her 50" flatscreen TV and listened to the news reports of four planes crashing into the three tallest buildings in the world which caused her chest to sink in because the love of her life just moved into one of those skyscrapers less than a month ago.

"Damnit, answer your damn phone boo!"

Aaliyah yelled as she repeatedly called her man's number, crying profusely as if her eyeballs were water-filled balloons being punctured by babies waving butcher knives.

After ten failed attempts Aaliyah ordered a car service to take her downtown to search for Tupac, and as she emerged from her building a disheveled Shakur was hopping out of a dingy, taxicab, running towards her.

"Baby girl I done been shot 9 times now they trying to blow me up!"

an animated 2pac said as he grabbed his gorgeous girlfriend in his arms and held her tight.

Aaliyah learned that when the first plane crashed into the north tower Tupac was still asleep but awakened when the 2nd plane struck the south tower.

He was able to gather himself and flee his building before the last two planes struck it simultaneously, one plane pounding into the 106th floor, while the other plane collided with the 59th floor, causing Tupac's tower to collapse much more quickly than it took the first towers to.

The deathless rapper didn't escape the toxic, dust clouds from the collapsing buildings though, which wreaked havoc on his one-lungless body, but he was able to catch a cab uptown to the love of his life on W. 57th street, so the labored breathing didn't really matter to him.

Section 7.7:

Westside!

Early into the following year, 'Pac's pleas to head west finally paid off and Aaliyah decided to leave New York for the sunny shores of Los Angeles.

The fortunate couple took up habitation in a Santa Monica beach house, gladdened that they escaped the terror of 9/11 and any possible repeat of the same trepidation.

A few days later God held a convention with His angels up in Heaven and the one named Alexis commented on how blessed her sister Aaliyah was to have had her earthly assignment extended, illustrating the fact that God the Father initially planned for the angel named Aaliyah to perish in a plane crash in the Bahamas in August 2001, but decided to switch His plans and appropriate her to be the help-meet of His son, Tupac Shakur, henceforth the pair got engaged and eventually tied the knot by the fall of that year.

Ever since Kidada passed his number to his boo, Tupac noticed several strange things about her that puzzled him like her constantly praying silently or looking upward at the ceiling, talking to God as if she could literally see Him, the same way he did when he cursed God out in his prison cell, so one hot night in their beachfront mansion he asked her if she really believed in God, and she said of course so he told her something he'd never told anyone else yet, save for his momma, which was that he was supposed to die back in 1996 but God saved him for a mission and he met a real live angel back then, on his deathbed.

The survivalist waited for his girl to start laughing at him or begin joking with him like she usually does but Aaliyah stunned him by not looking surprised or thinking he was talking crazy and spoke.

"Lemme guess who the angel was. Nathaniel right?"

"2pac reverted to the foul language he regularly used by saying "What in the fuck! How did u know that shit babe?"

Aaliyah laughed and revealed to him that she was actually an angel in the flesh too.

She used to make music with Satan in Heaven when he was named Lucifer, and God sent her down here for another purpose which is why she was scheduled to perish in a plane crash last year, but The Father gave her another assignment so here she is.

She further explained that Satan was using Foxy Brown to ruin God's plans, but Foxy isn't an evil person, so it was never going to work out.

2pac began drilling her with questions about what Heaven was like and is Jesus really white but she cut him short in her playful manner telling him that she can't answer those inquiries because they are G-14 classified, referencing the FBI's joke on the actor Chris Tucker's character in the film, *Rush Hour*.

'You play too damn much baby girl."

2pac blurted out gamesomely hitting her in the head with one of their sofa pillows.

This prompted her to affect a stern facial expression and end the subject on a more serious note by revealing that she honestly cannot tell him secret things about Heaven because he is still in human form and the information would overload his brain circuitry, but more importantly she would get into trouble with God and be taken off this assignment and sent back up to Heaven.

This news caused the Hail Mary rapper's heart to leap in his bullet-scarred chest because he loved Aaliyah more than he loved himself, so losing her would do what 9 bullets didn't do. Kill him.

Section 8

A few weeks later 'Pac was back in the five boroughs. His T.H.U.G. Life Ministries were there to help feed those affected by 9/11 as Thanksgiving approached.

His group passed out over 2000 turkeys which fed a lot of impoverished families that day.

On the final day of that trip, he was relaxing in his Times Square hotel room when his cell phone rang out. He quickly grabbed it, thinking it was his girl calling to update him about how her current tour was going, but surprisingly the voice of a rising rap star was heard on the other end.

"This sounds like the rapper 50 Cent. Is this you?"

A puzzled 'Pac asked wondering how the superstar got his number.

The muscular up-and-comer confirmed that it was him and that he had gotten his number from Mega-producer, Dr. Dre, with whom 2pac had made the 1995 hip hop hit called *California Love*, when Dre and he were still labelmates at Suge Knight's Death Row records.

After letting 'Pac know that he was his favorite artist of all time, Fifty spoke about his fresh deal with Shady/Aftermath Records, and how he was about to take over the rap game now that his first single,

Wanksta, was released two weeks ago and steadily shooting up the charts.

"Yeah, I don't listen to a lot of rap music these days unless it's my old shit," Tupac interjected

"But all I be hearing on the radio is that Wanksta song and I like that one."

He agreed causing 50 cent to smile through the phone.

The G-Unit general continued telling Tupac more about himself as Satan entered his mind and began to control it.

Although Curtis Jackson was a street-savvy hustler from the blocks of Southside, Jamaica, Queens, he wasn't as persuasive as the devil, therefore if 50 would've asked 'Pac to do a song feature for his upcoming album, the answer would have been a gentle no.

Because it was Satan using Curtis's mind, he was able to tempt Tupac with dozens of smooth words, and beneficial promises, one of which was Fif's wanting to sign him to his G-Unit records as its first artist.

2pac wasn't mentally or spiritually on the same level that Jesus Christ was on during his earthly expedition 2,000 years prior, when He also was tempted by the same devil so Shakur, just like the first woman on earth, Eve, fell victim to Satan's lies and agreed to all of 50 cent's requests.

Jesus Christ's mission was far greater than Tupac's mission, so his failure wasn't going to disrupt God's plans but imagine if Jesus Christ failed His mission too.

That's actually neither here nor there because you wouldn't even be alive reading this if it had.

So, 2pac and Satan ended their 2-hour phone session with 'Pac agreeing to meet 50 out in L.A. in a week to record his part for Fifty's first album single titled *In da club,* in which Dre wanted 'Pac to sing the chorus section of the song, which, in rap terms is called the hook.

During these recording sessions, Tupac wasn't as happy as others in the room due to Aaliyah and him fighting over his illogical decision to return to the rap game after doing interviews promising the world that he wasn't going to rap again after the Foxy Brown song.

"Do you work for God, or do you work for the devil?" she yelled at him when he first mentioned the news about his dealings with 50 cent and, having no real answer, told her that he is like The O.G.'s gangsta and will always put in work for the O.G. even when it doesn't look like he is.

"What's this O.G. stuff you're talking about? You back on that '90s gangsta bullshit again?"

The Grammy-winning singer asked, acting much wiser than her 23 years.

"No babe, O.G. means The Original God, The One God, or The Only God."

He explained, grabbing her hand and planting a delicate kiss on her knuckles.

2pac explained that the money he's making is going to his nonprofit so it's like taking the devil's money and using it for Godly use.

This explanation calmed her down enough to discontinue fighting with him but her body language throughout the next couple of days as he geared up for the *Get rich or die trying* album release let him know that she was still disappointed in him.

As 50 cent's first single and the album went to number 1 on several music charts there was a resurgence of demand for new music from the retired rapper.

50 cent's album marketing strategy also helped introduce 'Pac to a fresh generation of music fans when he mentioned in every interview that he was shot 9 times just like 'Pac was, and he survived those 9 bullet wounds the same as 'Pac did.

It was as if the immortality that 2pac possessed back in 1994 and 1996 was transferred to Curtis Jackson in 2000, allowing him to overcome what should have surely been a fatality.

The 32-year-old God-made-man found himself shoved back into the world's eyes as 50 cent's G-unit empire formed into a juggernaut.

His music catalog was revitalized as he accompanied Curtis on some of the biggest stages, and platforms in music, and you could hear cars on city streets blasting *Hit'em up* and *2 of Amerikaz most wanted* as if it was the mid-90s again.

'Pac was careful to bring Aaliyah along with him as often as he could, to fight the devil's attempts at temptation because it seemed like every female fan on the planet was being controlled by Satan to attempt to have sex with anyone and anything even remotely connected to 50 Cent and his G-Unit.

One night, after a live performance at B.E.T. network's *Spring Bling* concert, where the crowd went stark raving mad when 2pac burst out on stage singing the hook to *In da club* in his melodic, gravelly voice, as 50 followed with his first verse hanging upside down, Curtis and Shakur sat on a comfy sofa in 50's lavish tour bus as 50 elaborated on his plot to crush his arch-nemesis Ja Rule, a fellow Queens, N.Y. rapper with whom he felt is responsible for his shooting.

2pac listened closely to the words of revenge and plots and plans, and after Fif' finished talking he suggested that he forgive Ja and just keep moving forward with his career.

"Nigga you ain't the 'Pac I grew up listening to."

Curtis giggled as he playfully punched 'Pac on the shoulder.

2pac explained that the reason for his change is because of the O.G. which confused the new street rapper, who thought 'Pac was referring to an Original Gangster from the streets, which is an older street dude that is responsible for molding younger street dudes and teaching them not to make the same mistakes he has.

"No, nigga." Tupac laughed before elaborating on what the title O.G. stood for in his world.

Fifty was impressed with 2pac's explanation and from that point on began having more spiritual discussions with him which led to 50 penning a song for his second album which he named *God gave me style*, as well as writing lyrics for another song titled, *I'm supposed to die tonight* where he wrote lyrics about being confused as to whether he's God's child or Satan's angel.

The following year 50 released the first project on his G-Unit records, by his group *G-Unit*, which consisted of an incarcerated Tony Yayo, 50 cent, Young Buck, Lloyd Banks, and 2pac.

'Pac was highlighted more than the lesser-known artists on the project, despite some of them being childhood friends of 50's because the G-Unit general's plan of action was to prepare the world for the return of Makaveli Da Don.

2pac would assume this sub-name he used back in 1996, instead of his regularly used stage name of 2pac for his debut G-Unit album, because that old album was one of 50's favorites.

"We need to talk,"

Aaliyah said as Tupac came striding into their spacious bedroom after a long night at the studio.

"Sure, what's up babe?"

He replied as he leaned over and kissed her rosy lips.

"Damn bae you smell like you just came off of a marijuana farm,"

Aaliyah said shrinking back as she turned her head aside in disgust.

2pac laughed and told her all of the G-Unit artists and hangers-on in the studio smoke a lot of weed and the scent gets trapped in his clothing.

She then asked him if he remembers the part in the Holy Bible where the Apostle Paul claims to know someone who went up to Heaven for a visit, which he couldn't recall so she pulled his Bible out of the nightstand and opened it up.

"It's in 2nd Corinthians, chapter 12, verses 1-4."

She informed him before reading those verses aloud:

"It is doubtless not profitable for me to boast. I will come to visions and revelations of the Lord: I know a man in Christ who fourteen years ago---whether in the body I do not know, or whether out of the body I do not know, God knows---such a one was caught up to the third heaven. And I know such a man---whether in the body or out of the body I do not know, God knows---how he was caught up into Paradise and heard inexpressible words, which it is not lawful for a man to utter."

"Hold up."

A swift-thinking Tupac spoke.

"Are you saying what I think you're saying?"

Aaliyah just stared at him, and he suddenly knew that the same thing that happened to the person Paul referred to was about to happen to him.

"Oh shit, I'm about to see if Heaven has a ghetto."

He joyfully said, sourcing one of his old songs called *I wonder if Heaven got a ghetto.*

Aaliyah let him know that this isn't fun and games because when God the Father calls a human up to Paradise there is a major reason for doing so.

"Okay, I understand babe. So, when are we going?"

2pac asked soothingly, and before he could finish his question Aaliyah and he was sitting in white twin recliners in the middle of a white room the size of the Barclays Center in Brooklyn, New York.

"Yo babe where are we?"

2pac asked with glee in his eyes, excited to experience another miraculous act since it had been over half a decade since his first encounter with the angel Nathaniel.

"Is this Heaven?"

he finished before she broke it down to him that they were in proximity of Heaven but weren't technically inside of Heaven according to the Lord's measurements.

God used the room they were in as a conference room when interacting with humans.

The room sat just a few kilometers outside of the actual perimeter of what Almighty God considered to be Heaven.

Suddenly, a booming voice invaded the couple's ears as if they were leaning against huge, speaker boxes.

"Greetings Tupac and angel Aaliyah,"

God spoke in His distinctive baritone.

"Ohhh shit this is like that old flick the Wizard of Oz!"

Shakur said comically as his head shifted from left to right looking for the sight of God, causing Aaliyah to glare at him sharply.

"Oops, I'm sorry sir. I didn't mean to cuss."

He immediately realized that he used foul language in the presence of the Lord and regretted it instantly.

"It is alright son,"

God replied before elucidating a truth, which was that He never placed a curse on any of the words that humans consider cursed words and the notion that words like motherfucker, shit, and asshole are bad words derives from Satan's deception.

The humans who created those words were under the influence of the evil one to sway the world into accepting those words as bad but from a Heavenly standpoint, any word that a human uses to tear another one down is considered cursed at the time of usage.

"So, if you tell another human that they'll never amount to any-thing, using those exact words then you've just uttered cursed words, Tupac."

The Lord concluded.

"Wowww, that's deep sir."

Tupac blurted out.

"I never thought of it that way. ANY word, and not just the ones that are labeled cuss words can be cursed if we use them the wrong way."

A deep look of satisfaction rested on his face because of the Revelation he just learned, and Aaliyah glanced at him smiling, glad that her man had just received a great truth from Truth, Himself.

The Lord then moved away from the educational moment to the reason He summoned the human celebrity to a place that not too many humans will ever see while still alive on earth.

"So, angel Aaliyah, are you enjoying your time down there with the humans?"

God's vivid voice resonated throughout the large room as if a soundbar the size of an 18-wheeler's trailer was positioned behind them.

"Yes, it's okay my Lord, but I do miss Home though. Humans be acting extra sometimes." She responded.

"Well, I can always arrange for you to hop on another overloaded plane. You'll be back up here in time for dessert. Tonight, we're having angel cake."

The Lord's voice ruptured with roaring laughter that lasted several seconds.

This weird joke triggered anger in 2pac's thought process that he couldn't visibly hide, and he mentally asked why would the Lord say some dumb-ass shit like that about his wife?

It ain't shit funny about dying in a motherfuckin' plane crash!"

He continued yelling in his mind.

"You do know that I can read your thoughts right?" God informed Tupac.

"I'm sorry sir but that shit wasn't funny at all."

'Pac said as respectfully as he could under the circumstances because this was his first time learning that Aaliyah was supposed to die from a plane crash, but didn't because the Lord changed plans for her.

When God altered her path back in August 2001, no one knew about it except Him, so her human existence continued without incident, with no one being the wiser.

Aaliyah wasn't hurt by God's jesting though because angels are accustomed to the Lord's ways and aren't shocked when He does things that humans would find unbelievable, like ordering the death of an infant the same way He did in The Holy Bible's Book of 2nd Samuel, Chapter 12, verses 14 through 18.

As Aaliyah rubbed 'Pac's hand soothingly, calming him down a crack of thunder suddenly deafened 'Pac's ears as if someone purposely turned the volume up on a lightning sound effects YouTube video.

"Now, you see how upset you are at the thought of me ordering angel Aaliyah's plane to crash?"

God's query bellowed out with a sharp tone in his voice.

"Well, I am 10 times angrier at you for signing a damn recording contract with that G-unit Curtis Jackson human!"

2pac's frown lines started softening as fright began creeping into his psyche.

"I did NOT save your life TWICE for you to still be rapping in the human year of 2004 and if you don't cease all music activities immediately this is what I'll do to you!"

Section 9:

Hell

Instantly, Tupac was struggling to stay afloat in a fiery lake.

It was as if there was a huge gasoline spill and someone flicked a half-smoked Newport cigarette on its surface, igniting it instantly.

The strange thing is that 'Pac was being burned alive, but his skin was not melting off as it should be, although he did feel tremendous pain from the flames.

And the smell hovering above the burning water caused him to vomit.

The closest thing he could think of to the stench was the time he saw a decaying, dead body, in the back of a dilapidated building when he first relocated to California as a teenager.

He still recalls that smell, and the squirming maggots that were feasting on its decomposing flesh that steamy, July evening.

"I'm sorry God, Helllppp!"

Tupac yelled out as he felt his wiry arms losing strength. After fighting for a few more seconds, he felt something wrap around his right leg and begin dragging him towards what looked like the shore, but he wasn't sure because of the 3-foot-high flames obscuring most of his view.

As they got closer to land whatever was latched onto his leg began emerging from the hot water becoming more visible.

A frightened Tupac nearly defecated on himself at the sight of the brutish creature that continued dragging him by one tentacle.

The beast was a blend of a wolf spider mixed with an octopus, but it had the head of a wild boar, only with 5 fierce eyeballs planted in its face.

Shakur suffered from arachnophobia when dealing with small, household spiders so being this close to an 8-foot-tall half spider raised his blood pressure, and anxiety tremendously.

He started screaming at the top of his lungs like a middle school girl being abducted by force.

Then, the smelly creature opened its 4 tentacles, and 4 spider legs, showing off its 19-foot wingspan, revealing what resembled an extremely hairy human vagina.

The monster then used one of its tentacles to form the letter 'O' and one of its spider legs to stroke the circular limb in and out, in a sexual motion.

"Come fuck me 2pac."

The beast gurgled the words out in a husky, torn voice before wrapping a tentacle around a petrified 'Pac and pulling his body towards its soggy womb.

Totally exhausted, Tupac began suffering from heart palpitations as his face was plunged into the beast's pussy and the only thought that he could form, as a gooey substance began drowning him, was that he was literally ingesting human feces.

"Wake up babe."

A familiar soft voice repeated over and over but he could barely hear it because it sounded like someone had turned the volume down to its lowest setting.

Tupac slowly opened his swollen eyes to a vision of white blurriness, as a light-skinned hand with lavender purple fingernails lightly slapped his face on each cheek.

"Yo, those are my wife's nails."

Tupac thought and then he remembered what had happened and forced himself to fully awaken.

Eyes filled with tears; an exhausted Tupac began an attempt to tell Aaliyah what he had just undergone.

"I know, I know babe I was watching you on the jumbotron,"

she said motioning for him to look upward at an actual jumbotron that wasn't in the humongous white room before his involuntary excursion to hell, replaying the scene of him trying to stay afloat in the blazing, body of water before being dragged ashore.

"I damn near died, babe!"

'Shakur said before the Lord chimed in and explained to him that the encounter, he just had isn't even close to a fraction of what it's going to be like in Hell and that he should obey His command and leave the music alone and focus on doing more positive stuff, so he'll never get a chance to get that full experience.

This prompted 'Pac to get down on his hands and knees and bow down to an invisible pair of feet in front of him and promise the Lord that he willfully obeys Him from now on and mere seconds after mouthing his heartfelt prayer and promise, Aaliyah and he was instantly teleported back into the bedroom of their beachside mansion.

Section 8.8

Holding his chest as if his heart was still in a Nascar race, Tupac looked at his wife and spoke.

"I'm 'bout to call this nigga 50. It's OVER!"

That phone call didn't transpire too well and resulted in the new rapper with the juggernaut-backing threatening the older rapper with a lawsuit that his bank account couldn't handle.

It turns out that 2pac's attorneys were able to get him released from his contract with G-unit and Interscope records thanks to the relationship he had with music giant, Jimmy Iovine who gave him his first recording contract back in 1991, after founding Interscope a year prior.

This incensed Curtis and later caused him to terminate his conjunction with Interscope and seek distribution elsewhere.

2pac was even allowed to keep his 8 million dollar signing bonus, which further outraged Fifty who began plotting on ruining the Thug Life rapper's reputation in the same fashion that he did with fellow Queens emcee Ja Rule, via diss songs he began recording that would appear on his sophomore album the following year.

Aaliyah and 'Pac was cruising to the Crenshaw Christian Center in South Central, L.A. when a new song aired on the hip hop station they regularly listened to.

"Clickety-clank, Clickety-clank."

The chorus began with 50 cent's distinctive voice then dived into his disrespectful verses of notable rappers, primarily 2pac whom he rapped that the Thug Lifer took 9 shots like him but now he's sucking God's dick making the gangstas sick.

Aaliyah, driving their Bentley Arnage glanced over at her man who had a menacing snarl on his face which prompted her to warn him about what would happen to him if he retaliated.

Tupac was forced to sit back and try to disregard the media coverage that 50 received from the record, recalling the night he spent in Hell which was far worse than being dissed on a song and not retaliating.

2pac endured the backlash that the media forced his way from the popularity of 50's song as well as the other 2 diss tracks that the embittered rapper included on his *Massacre* LP, but 'Pac slowly got over the negativity, mainly fueled by fear of God which moved him to seek higher ground.

That opportunity arrived when he was driving downtown one muggy summer day and passed by the Los Angeles headquarters of U.S. Senator Dianne Feinstein.

He zeroed in on the signs hanging from the large office windows urging voters to keep the long-lasting senator in office by voting next year.

Literally, a light bulb popped on in 'Pac's brain and he decided right then and there that he would try to be a positive influence on others by becoming a U.S. Senator and even the first black president of the United States if he could go that far.

He grabbed his iPhone and spewed out his plans to his beloved wife as he sped home so he could research what the requirements were to run for a U.S Senate spot in 2006.

Being a Democratic voter since he was of age to go to the polls, Shakur easily decided to run as a Dem' which meant he had to go to war with the very same woman whose campaign ads inspired him to give it a go in the first place. Dianne Feinstein.

Section 9:

Suit & tie shit

In the remaining months of 2005, Tupac used a portion of his wealth, $7 million big ones to be exact to hit the streets and jumpstart his campaign for the U.S. senate.

He also combined promotion through his nonprofit to give out thousands of pounds of food and clothing to the poor.

His wife Aaliyah, who was at this time a multiple-Grammy Award-winning artist performed charity concerts that benefited hundreds of thousands of civilians in Los Angeles County which increased 'Pac's popularity numbers.

Most of the media were using the former rapper's gangster past to disparage him but his Ministry's benevolence overshadowed those negative news reports because the people were pleased with his current efforts and not his past exploits.

"Barack, come here, you're not going to believe this!"

An astonished woman shrieked as her eyeballs stayed cemented to the plasma TV monitor in her Georgetown living room.

Her husband, Illinois senator, Barack Obama plopped the last bite of a homemade taco into his mouth before exiting their kitchen to see why his wife was so excited.

They tuned in as Tupac appeared on an episode of 'Larry King Live', revealing that he was joining the senate race in California.

"Doesn't he know that there's a process to this thing?" Barack spoke aloud.

"I was a frickin' state senator when I lost an election,"

Obama said, referring to his year 2000 defeat at the hands of four-term incumbent Bobby Rush.

The Obamas spent the rest of that night marveling at the fact that a former gangsta rapper-turned Christian decided to stop making music to become a high-level politician.

"Who the hell is 2pac?"

Senator Feinstein asked her campaign manager one afternoon, pronouncing the former rapper's name *Two-Pack*.

The thirty-, something-year-old administrator happily filled his aging boss in on who the musical icon is, primarily because he loved 'Pac's body of work, especially the *Me against the world* CD.

The hard-nosed assemblywoman wasn't at all pleased with the L.A. Times newspaper article she had just read about a possible primary election blooming due to Shakur's strengthening movement.

Because of Shakur's celebrity, he was able to book appearances on morning and night shows, from Good Morning America to Jimmy Kimmel Live, humorously highlighting that he should be the next senator from California because he is the only person running that made a state anthem, referencing his hit collaboration with mega-producer Dr. Dre.

Shakur's eloquence, determination, and wit helped his numbers rise drastically, causing more Californians to take notice of his campaign promises, and strategies to make America greater than it already was by shaking Washington up with fresh blood.

Aaliyah was cuddling in the living room with California's possible future senator, when a campaign ad commercial appeared on their TV screen, sponsored by Senator Feinstein, calling attention to Tupac's violent past.

The commercial covered him shooting 2 off-duty cops in Atlanta to him getting shot 4 times in a Vegas drive-by.

These tactics were seemingly damaging but didn't work out in the Feinstein camp's favor because when the Democratic primary was held that spring Tupac beat out the veteran politician by 1,453,044 votes, to become the primary Democratic candidate from the State of California to run for a Senate seat.

The job didn't stop there, and Shakur treated the victory as if he lost the election.

The same force that drove the slender man to record over 2000 songs in a short span of time also drove him to continue campaigning hard to ensure a big win when the general election rolled around that November.

The B.E.T. network called Shakur and Aaliyah a week later to ask if they would like to be presenters at their award show next month and they gladly accepted the invitation, both having received B.E.T. awards for their musical projects.

Section 9

On the night of the star-studded event, they decided to twin wearing matching outfits that their friend Kidada picked out for them.

"Do you believe in God?"

An excited Tupac asked the crowded hall as he and Aaliyah stood at the podium midway through the show, multiple cameras broadcasting the affair live.

"Well believe in Senator Shakur!"

Tupac jokingly finished before presenting Southern rapper-T.I.-with the album of the year award.

The laughter was uproarious as most of the people in the auditorium realized that 'Pac had just stolen his own question from a decade earlier when he posed a similar query to promote his short-lived record label *Death Row East*.

During the following month's candidate, Shakur and his team continued campaigning diligently across the state visiting major cities like San Francisco and San Diego, as well as smaller towns like Sausalito and Palm Springs elaborating on 'Pac's agenda to help change the country through fresh legislation.

Tupac's campaign slogan was

'Time to heal each other',

which derived from lyrics he penned back in the '90s for a song called *Changes*.

He shouted those words out at the end of every speech he made on the trail and by the time the general election arrived millions of Californians believed in the necessity to put those words into action.

"Ladies and gentlemen, we are still waiting on a few polling places to turn in their votes in the states of Nevada, Florida, and California."

CNN's Lou Dobbs reported live during his show's coverage of the mid-term elections.

"Man, this is some bullshit!"

An irate 'Pac shouted slamming his empty bottle of beer on the ground, near his feet, causing it to shatter into pieces.

"I done put in all this work and spent all this money for nothing!"

"Babe chill out!"

His angelic spouse said consoling him with her melodic voice as she began hugging him as the roomful of his campaign team watched in silence.

Senator Feinstein was beating Tupac by 1,504 votes and if most of the remaining ballots weren't for Shakur then she will come out victorious by a narrow margin.

As the suspense rose in the large office room Tupac and his group sat around another 45 minutes chattering and waiting on Dobbs to report some favorable news when he finally came back on the air after a commercial break and mouthed the words

"Well, it looks like California has a new senator."

Which caused a shocked Shakur to grab his girl by the face with both hands and kiss her pouty lips before hopping up off the office couch he was sunk in and bursting out in song and dance.

"California...knows how to party."

A jubilant Shakur sang as someone turned his old song on the office's stereo system, as he crip walked in the middle of the frenzy as his team members all danced and celebrated as they eyed the official numbers on the TV screen.

Shakur finished with just 237 more votes than the long-tenured Dianne Feinstein, making him the first hip hop senator in Washington D.C.

Needing time to de-stress after running a hard-fought political campaign 'Pac and Aaliyah went on a vacation to the Bahamas.

The sexy singer had fallen in love with the island after shooting her *Rock the boat* video there eons ago and considered the place a second home.

After a few weeks in the Caribbean, the couple jetted off to the Amalfi coast to wrap up their winter vacay before returning to California to pack their bags for their new residence in Washington.

"Back to this brick-ass weather."

Senator Shakur mouthed as he stepped out of the back of his black chauffeured Chevy Tahoe.

The temperature was 19 degrees as the suited-up rookie made his way into the Hart Senate office building where an office was set up for him to begin his new career.

After being introduced to his new duties and getting familiarized with the new surroundings he made his way to the building's cafeteria for lunch.

After taking a second bite of a juicy cheeseburger as he sat alone at one of the café's tables someone placed a hand on his right shoulder, followed by words from a voice that commanded your attention.

"Hey Tupac, how are you doing today brother?"

Newly elected Senator, Barack Obama said as he sat down next to his fellow African American statesman, taking a bite into his chicken & bacon ranch sub sandwich.

Obama introduced himself and revealed that he was a first-year senator who learned the ropes around D.C. quickly, encouraging Shakur to come to him if he needed any help navigating the white world of Washington politics.

The pair soon became friends, despite a decade age difference, and regularly double-dated when they took their women out on the town.

Section 9:

Eyes on the big house

A year into his senatorship Shakur began fulfilling his promise of changing the world by introducing a bill in the Chamber of Congress which he named the *Blue Screen Bill*.

The main reason for the new law would be to filter out bad cops from good cops and this was something dear to 'Pac's heart, having won a civil lawsuit around age twenty after Oakland P.D. officers assaulted and arrested him for jaywalking.

The highlight of the legislation is that all police academies cadets- nationwide- undergo a polygraph test with one of the primary questions being

"Do you hate people of other races, whether it be their skin color or their ways?"

There will be a series of other questions included in the lie detector exam that would assist in weeding out potential racist officers who would misuse their authority on certain suspects.

Senator Shakur's bill was the high point of several CNN and Fox News segments but after months of discussion the day came for it to be voted into power and it failed to receive enough votes.

Shortly after this disappointment Tupac's Senate homie Obama, announced his intentions to run for the presidency in 2008 raising eyebrows everywhere.

"Yooo, you really gon' run for that shit?"

'Pac asked Barack as they sat at their favorite table in their building's cafeteria, munching on Chinese food.

"Most definitely."

Barack began replying, wiping egg roll crumbs from his mouth.

"I talked it over with Michelle and we're gonna give it a shot."

He finished his sentence before 'Pac jumped in.

"Hey, I know you gonna put ya boy down if you make it right?"

Which prompted Obama to reply by saying he, himself, had a long shot in hell of winning the presidency but someone with a background the size of Tupac's didn't have a snowball's chance in Hell of holding a presidential position which caused them both to break out in laughter as a group of white Republican senators passed by their table wearing expressions of conceit on their faces.

As junior-senator Obama ramped up promotion of his presidential bid Tupac saw less of his cohort and continued focusing on introducing new laws that would aid in changing the climate of the country.

Section 9.3

As the summer months began winding down Satan began mentally assaulting Tupac in an attempt to bring him back over to the dark side.

"Yes, we can."

Obama's smooth baritone blared out through the plasma TV speakers, as he wrapped up another campaign speech.

Aaliyah turned off the Panasonic TV in their bedroom, as Tupac lay in bed harboring jealousy.

"Haven't even seen that nigga in a week and we supposed to be boys!"

Shakur blurted out into the sudden silence of the room.

After a few minutes of his wife coaxing him 'Pac revealed that he was holding feelings of resentment towards his Washington buddy and wished he could be in his spot.

This caused Aaliyah to revert to the Heavenly side of her personality and scold her man for exhibiting envy for what God has blessed someone with instead of staying focused on impressing the Lord with good works.

She ended the conversation that night by telling Tupac to simply ask Barack if he would allow him to be his running mate.

If he rejected the request then it is God's Will, but if he accepted the request it is also God's Will.

A restless Shakur allowed his wife's words to settle in his thought process as he drifted off to sleep that night but the following morning those same words caused a determined Tupac to implement a plan of action.

Dripping sweat from a game of 3-on-3 in the basement gym of the Hart Senate building, Obama hit the showers and was standing at his locker, with the door ajar as he scrambled through the clutter searching for his stick of deodorant.

After finding the speed stick and rubbing its sweet-scented chalk on his armpits, he closed his locker door jumping back in astonishment as a steely-eyed Tupac appeared behind the door as if he was a ghost.

"Damn, you scared the shit outta me Tupac." Obama stammered as he pulled a t-shirt over his head.

"I ain't seen you in a while so I'm just checkin' on you potnah,"

'Pac replied, mispronouncing the word 'partner' in his New York-slash-California accent.

"Hey, Hey wait a minute. Are we filming Juice part 2? "

Obama asked chuckling, referencing 2pac's role in the 1992 movie *Juice*, where his character popped up on actor, Omar Epps's character at their high school, after a period of not seeing each other for a spell.

After a moment of quietness, the pair both broke out guffawing because they genuinely loved each other and were happy for the present reunion.

'You my nigga Barack." Tupac blurted out.

"Let me run with you."

He asked in a manner of speaking requesting that Obama make him his presidential running mate.

"Now, you know I love you like a brother Tupac, but do you really think the people are going to cast their vote for, not one but two Black dudes next year?"

"We're just gonna have to wait until November 4th of next year to see!" Shakur replied.

"Aren't you the same dude that said we ain't ready to have a Black president?"

Obama countered.

"Nigga, I wrote that shit over ten years ago. Times have changed."

Tupac completed his sentence, laughing before furthering the discourse between his friend and him, eventually convincing Barack that they could win the ultimate prize despite his violent background.

Obama officially announced that Senator Shakur would be his running mate at a press conference in his adopted hometown of Chicago.

This news disappointed his initial pick Senator Joe Biden of Delaware who was expected to receive the pick after dining with the Obamas a week prior and laying out what he would bring to the table as a veteran politician.

The Obama-Shakur ticket became the media's main topic of discussion as the duo campaigned harder than either of them ever did in their political lives to make it to the White House.

Obama's opponent, Senator John McCain was a crafty military veteran who made it a point to highlight the surnames of his challengers during various campaign speeches, which sparked controversy in the media.

"Osama Bin Laden, Barack Obama."

"Osama, Obama."

Osama Bin Laden, the culprit responsible for the 9/11 terrorist attacks had a first name that was similar to Senator Obama's last name, and this rubbed some people the wrong way just as Senator Shakur's name did.

Section 10

Back in the 1970s, a woman by the name of Assata Shakur was involved in the shooting death of a New Jersey State trooper.

After being sent to prison for the crime Shakur's supporters helped break her out of prison and get her transported down to the island nation of Cuba where she lives in exile.

Although she doesn't share ties of kindred with Senator Shakur she is his godmother, thanks to Afeni Shakur giving her that title after his birth in 1971.

As the election year continued rolling forward both senators received vocal support from silver screen celebrities the likes of Robert DeNiro, Denzel Washington, Will Smith, and several more to musicians like Stevie Wonder and Nas.

These well-known people professing the approval of Obama helped common people love the man's agenda even more.

Obama's three core issues were to end the Iraqi war, provide universal healthcare to all Americans, and increase energy independence all of which he hammered home at the presidential debates allowing him easy victories in each of them.

His running mate had it too easy in his debate with Alaskan Governor Sarah Palin who came across as a dumb blonde with brunette-colored hair.

Tupac revealed one of his VP goals was to work with the future president to introduce a new law banning the subjects of sex, drugs, and gun violence from all genres of music.

This notion had been lingering in the back of his mind for months now because even though he was a gangsta rapper at one time he had changed and was displeased with the way the art form called rap was shifting into being totally about negativity.

Throughout the night Governor Palin kept reviving the details of his wild past but Americans remembered it all and weren't going to let those reminders affect their voting.

Obama swept through his three debates with clear victories and Tupac did the same ending the Vice-Presidential discourse, reminding viewers that he has learned a lot from operating his nonprofit organization and will apply those skills to his position under Obama.

After a bumpy year and a half of campaigning election day finally arrived and by the end of the night, Obama and Shakur were granted the titles of President and Vice President-Elect.

The president spent the first year of his first term growing more gray hairs as his *Affordable Care Act* stalled in Congress but finally reached approval in the fall of 2009.

Barack felt good to accomplish this major goal. History has shown that most U.S. Vice-Presidents aren't usually mentioned much during their tenure, but VP Shakur disrupted that regularity when he submitted another mention-worthy bill to congress in the middle of his first term named the *Vulgar Vocalism* Bill which would disallow musicians from using lyrics about drugs, violence, guns, and sex in their lyrics.

When the media first caught wind of this desired law Tupac received tremendous backlash on social media largely due to his own background.

One journalist who went viral complained that the man who was responsible for most of the negative influences in rap music is now trying to turn against it.

Upon becoming vice-president 2pac deleted his *Facebook* account therefore, several celebrities and rappers, who had yet to start using the fairly new social media application named *Twitter* began signing up for it so they could message him and express their distaste for his proposed bill which, if passed in the House would change the landscape of music forever.

The word 'hypocrite' was used a lot in the millions of direct messages the vice-president began receiving.

After months of continued criticism, debate, and news media coverage *The Vulgar Vocalism* bill

was voted on and passed through the House of Representatives and the Senate floor rapidly because VP Shakur revealed in various interviews and speeches that he was still mentally suffering from the death of a Texas State trooper, back in 1992 who was shot and killed by a teen in a stolen car while listening to his first album, "2pacalypse now."

At his trial, the teen's attorney claimed that 2pac's lyrics, many of which were laced with violence against law enforcement motivated the teen to shoot the officer.

Some of the members of the House and Senate recalled this event and were touched by the maneuver that the VP was making to right his wrongs and this helped them to quickly cast their votes.

2pac burst through the Oval office doors walking the same way he did on the night he led the attack at the MGM Grand casino in Vegas.

"I'm not signing that shit Tupac!"

President Obama's velvety baritone voice flowed throughout the commodious room.

"What 'chu mean you ain't signin' it Barack! Why you vetoing my shit!?"

Tupac countered with aggression in his voice as he stood over the seated president who shoved some papers into a file folder before rising from his plush chair.

"I'm the president of the United States so you better sit your little ass down with all of this attitude Tupac!"

An inflamed Obama unusually shouted as his 6'2" frame towered over 2pac's by nearly a half-foot.

"If I signed this damn bill it would affect millions of lives. There are a lot of families being fed off of the proceeds from rap music."

He said matter-of-factly before sitting back down.

"I mean, what in the hell would people like Lil Wayne or Snoop Dogg rap about it if they couldn't talk about sex and drugs?"

The two friends went back and forth arguing about the importance of the bill compared to the backlash it was receiving from a great portion of the American population.

President Obama even reminded his VP that his approval ratings had dropped by 37% since introducing the controversial bill due to his connection to him which could affect their chances of a second term the following year.

Obama remained firm in his decision causing Tupac to reluctantly accept the fact that his bill would never become law.

The termination of Osama Bin Laden months later aided in smoothing things over, and the Obama-Shakur ticket easily won a second term which turned out to be more eventful than the first.

The president was able to withdraw more troops from Afghanistan, win a fight with Republicans over his Homeland Security bill, and normalize relations with the country Cuba which allowed many Americans including his friends Beyonce and Jay-Z to visit the island nation after travel restrictions were lifted from over a half-century ago.

The more eventful part of Obama's second term came in the latter part of his incumbency.

Hamza Bin Laden, the son of Osama Bin Laden who was present the day Seal Team Six executed his dad in his third-floor bedroom vowed to get revenge on Barack for having his father killed.

Hamza was groomed by his dad to hate America and rose in the ranks of Al-Qaeda after his father's death.

By early 2016 he became second-in-command to Ayman al-Zawahiri, The leader of the terrorist group.

The zealous young man used his power to form a special group of Al-Qaeda commandos to help him kidnap the president of the United States, on a trip he was planning on taking in March, according to CNN.

An unwilling Zawahiri refused to take part in the abduction but did nothing to thwart Hamza's objectives assuring him that he loved his father as much as him but revealing that the organization didn't have the proper number of resources to stave off a U.S. military response.

Osama's blood-thirsty son wasn't concerned with a lack of resources and was overly eager to avenge the murder of his beloved dad, A man that taught him everything including hating America more than he did.

Section 11:

New rapper emerges

"I still see your shadows it's too soon." A teenager with a melodic voice rapped into his iPhone before deleting the recording.

The Soundcloud rapper named *JuicetheKidd* was sitting in his bedroom attempting to write the lyrics to a song in an effort to make a huge hit.

The 17-year-old pianist grunted in frustration as he racked his brain for lyrics to the song he was working on, which he titled *Lucid Nightmares.*

"Chill Juice, that's too much bro! You're gonna OD!"

One of the rapper's closest friends said as Jarad shoved a handful of Percocet pills into his mouth as if they were canned cashews.

Jarad was a heavy drug user and dabbled in everything from Xanax to a purple-colored drink called *Lean,* which is a concoction of cough syrup, sprite, and hard candy.

'Maaan this ain't shit. I've taken more than this before."

Jarad barked back as he grabbed his iPad and logged into his Soundcloud account to check his artist stats.

"This is some bullshit!"

The frustrated rapper said with a depressed look on his face as he saw that he had only gotten 2 listens for his latest uploaded track.

"No one is fucking with my music on here!

Juice's friends all racked their brains for something he could do to change his luck when one of them suggested that he change his name and focus more on the Emo-rap he was doing.

Another friend suggested that he pattern himself after another Soundcloud artist who began garnering a lot of attention the year before.

"You and XXXTentacion kinda like the same shit anyway bro'."

A slender teen named Kevin said as he turned on Jarad's bedroom TV.

"He listens to that rock & roll shit just like you and talks about suicide and all of that crazy shit."

"Riverside Mothafucka!"

2pac's character snarled in the 1992 classic urban film named Juice before shooting his nemesis to death in a murky alley.

"That's it!"

A peppy Jarad said enthusiastically as his friends all stared at the TV marveling at how gangster the vice-president of the United States was back in the '90s.

He then explained to his friends that he was going to change his moniker from *JuicetheKidd* to *JuiceWRLD* because he was about to take over the world with the advice they had given him.

In the following months, the determined Chicago emcee worked on his craft releasing a series of singles and mixtapes, creating a buzz that gained the attention of a few record labels.

He decided to sign a contract with 2pac's first label, Interscope records because Jimmy Iovine offered the most money the teen had ever dreamed of receiving at one time.

The emo rapper's substance abuse increased now that his bank account gained a little weight, but it didn't affect him from working on the songs that would appear on his debut album the following year.

Section 11:

Sneaky

"Back in the Holy land."

The president said as he disembarked from Air Force One and climbed into the rear of his black Cadillac limousine which had been transported along with a dozen other Government vehicles in a ginormous C-17 aircraft as is the custom when a U.S. President travels abroad.

After paying his respects, and letting the Israelis know that he loved them Obama's entourage made the trek eastward over to the country of Jordan where he hadn't been since a voyage there three years prior when he toured the ancient city of Petra.

On this trip, the Secret Service decided to bed the President down in a different hotel than on the previous trip for obvious safety reasons.

Little did they know Hamza Bin Laden monitored their every move thanks to spies that he planted at Queen Alia International Airport who immediately reported when the President's plane landed and gave minute-by-minute updates until his group was given the intel on where the President's destination was.

U.S. Presidents and other high-ranking officials travel in what the American media has dubbed *"A regal bubble."*

Barack Obama was appreciative of this protective bubble due to being the most traveled President in U.S. history, having already made 50 plus trips to nearly 60 countries.

Just like all previous trips, his entourage consisted of the inclusion of press, Secret Servicemen, and aides, all of whom had strict guidelines to adhere to.

For this visit, just like all previous ones Secret service agents had already staked out the town and surrounding area, months prior going over every possible scenario if an attack occurred.

The Secret Service's counter-assault squad carried enough KAC SR-25s and FN P90 submachine guns to mow down a large village and was fully prepared to lay down an ample amount of suppressive gunfire if needed.

The entire hotel was cleared out days ago as the U.S. Government footed the exorbitant bill to rent every room in the 6-story structure.

This safety measure assured that no unknowns would be able to occupy the building during the president's stay.

Hamza knew that kidnapping a U.S. president was not going to be an easy goal to meet but he was cut from the same cloth as the man who unbelievably pulled off the first major attack on America's mainland so his faith in himself, after years of being trained and groomed by a monster-in-human flesh motivated him to continue with his machinations until the time to strike arrived.

For the past four years, he and his group trained and practiced their positions for the day that the abduction would finally happen.

On one of these hot and sweaty days of simulation one of Hamza's men asked him what he was going to do with Obama when they captured him.

"I don't know yet my friend. He's not the actual man that killed my father but because he is America's leader I'll definitely have to behead him."

The bitter man replied as he wiped down the barrel of an AK-47 rifle with an oily gray rag.

I think I'll have a little fun first though. Make some outlandish demands and make those western infidels worry a little." He finished his sentences with a grin before cocking his rifle and letting off a barrage of gunfire striking his paper target where its head and penis would have been if it were a person.

Section 10.5

Two years later President Obama extended his basketball player legs out of the rear of his limo as heavily armed agents mobilized and surrounded him for his entrance into the Jordanian hotel.

"Damn it's cold out here tonight." He said glancing at a few of his security detail.

"I thought we were in the Country of Jordan, but it feels like you mothafuckas have me back in Chicago and I'm about to go see Michael Jordan."

The ever-joking Obama elicited an eruption of laughter from the agents as they made their way up the sidewalk to the side entrance of the grand establishment.

Milliseconds later several missile silos landed and detonated in various spots around the hotel grounds causing an odorless gas to disperse rapidly, rendering everyone in its path unconscious.

"Get the gas masks now!"

one Secret Service agent shouted to another as they relied on their chemical warfare training to kick in and assist them in getting the situation under control.

Hamza's scheme was working thanks to his usage of *space blankets* made of Mylar foil to conceal the seven different rocket launchers his men used to deliver the sleeping gas-laden missiles.

The Pentagon's space station allowed government forces to track any movement on planet earth, but the son of Osama was still able to deploy these rockets without interference.

Bin Laden's missiles contained a mixture of incapacitating agents that were more of a riot-control variety than a kill all these American heathens' assortment.

The young leader was smart enough to know that abducting a standing U.S. President was going to draw heat that Hell didn't even know about but pulling it off without any casualties would lessen the blow and his army achieved that task by wounding only four Secret Servicemen who weren't fully affected by the fumes and attempted to terminate the threat.

Hamza's men grabbed a slumped over Obama off the cool pavement and shoved him inside of a waiting vehicle, as they all executed their plan just as they had been training to do so the past couple of years.

No one died that night, but the United States of America and King Abdullah II of Jordan suffered a terrible embarrassment for allowing a visiting dignitary to get kidnapped, something that had never happened before in U.S. history, save for your occasional American President movie.

"Bae wake up!"

Aaliyah yelled as she shook a snoring Tupac, who hadn't fully gotten rid of his liquor demons, partaking in a little too much Hennessy the night before.

The Vice-President shot up in his bed in a semi-drunken stupor and attempted to assess what his wife was saying.

"The Secret Service has knocked on the door 5 times and your phone has been blowing up for the past 10 minutes. It better not be no bitch."

She finished with a threatening tone in her voice, still not used to the Government's strict protocol of her, or anyone else not being allowed to go through her man's phone due to his position in the government.

"Daaamn, chill out babe. You know damn well I ain't got no Monica's in my office."

Tupac laughed, referencing the Monica Lewinsky and Bill Clinton scandal two decades earlier as he ran to the bedroom door of their Northwest D.C. mansion and opened it to bad news.

Tupac's regular security detail greeted him, in addition to their supervisors, as well as generals from the Pentagon.

They all filled him in on the details of the disastrous night in Jordan, on top of the heartbreaking news that his mother just suffered a cardiac arrest, which caused her to succumb to an attack on her heart.

For the first time in his 45 years on earth, a half-drunken overwhelmed Tupac Shakur fainted into unconsciousness like a damsel in distress.

"Bae wake up!"

Tupac's beautiful wife said as she hovered over him, her tears dropping into his dry mouth like raindrops.

"Sir, we have to swear you in ASAP!"

a general announced sternly, as a dizzy Shakur slowly began to rise.

Due to President Obama being taken hostage in Jordan hours earlier, Vice-President Tupac Shakur was sworn in as the 45th President of the United States of America.

What sliced the new President's heart in half was his mother, the woman that helped mold him, who didn't get a chance to see his significant moment due to going into cardiac arrest and later expiring at a local hospital.

"At least she saw me become vice-president but damn momma I'm the President now."

The presently depressed-yet-excited Commander-in-Chief thought to himself as he sat in his friend's office chair being briefed on current developments in his abduction.

"Osama Bin Laden's son is the one behind this Mr. President!"

A stern general blurted out as he stood in front of a group of other Pentagon officials.

The assembly explained that they have tracked Obama's location thanks to the GPS microchip that was implanted inside of his left arm's dermis after his inauguration.

Government scientists created the chip two decades earlier and first used it during Clinton's second term, continuing usage with every U.S. President onward in the event of an abduction.

"Well, I need y'all to set up a phone call with that buster!" The current Head of State said in his gravelly voice reverting to a slang word from his younger years ready to do whatever it took to liberate his friend Barack.

Section 11

The groggy man began regaining consciousness as his blurry eyes concentrated on focusing on any object that appeared before them.

After a few more minutes of being self-resuscitated a clear-minded Obama fully awakened to the scene of him being handcuffed to a steel chair in a dimly lit room, with several men standing in its shadows, guarding him.

"Hey fellas, how y'all doing?" a diplomatic-thinking Barack Obama mouthed before Hamza Bin Laden emerged from the shapes, back-hand slapping the smooth-talking statesman on the left side of his face hard enough to cause a small degree of whiplash.

After a few minutes to clear the fuzziness out of his head, Barack continued his plea.

"Now, wait for a minute brother. I know who you are. I recognize you from the intel that my generals presented to me a while ago."

He said, cocking his head to the right as if that movement would alleviate the pain in his neck.

"I didn't kill your dad but- "

Obama's appeal was cut short by one of Hamza's overzealous followers wrapping his muscular bicep around the President's neck and choking him quiet.

As the American chief squirmed in his uncomfortable chair Hamza pushed his man away forcefully reminding him that he didn't want the world to see a battered U.S. President, even though he had just slapped the man hard enough to leave a red mark on his face.

Section 11.4:

Seventeen Days

A few days after burying his beloved mother in Marin County where he first touched California soil the Pentagon finally connected the new President with Hamza Bin Laden via a satellite phone call.

"Hey, Mr. Tupac this is the son of Osama Bin Laden you're talking to."

Hamza began the conversation by finishing his introduction with a few demands like the release of all inmates from Guantanamo Bay removing all troops from the middle east, a money wire of 500 million dollars to an offshore bank account, and having a statue of his dad erected, to replace the Statue of Liberty in New York City.

As 'Pac sat listening to the younger Bin Laden his inner thug resurfaced, and he interjected the kidnapper's talking with a rant.

"Now I done already told yo' ass it was just about Osama, then all you middle east mothafuckas had to open y'all mouths so this is how we doing this shit. Fuck Al-Qaeda as a terrorist group and staff. Fuck you Hamza Bin Laden you can die slow bitch ass nigga! My fo' fo' make sho' all yo' mark ass soldiers die slow! You mothafuckas can't see us or be us! Out here in America, we bomb on mothafuckas!"

The President yelled into the phone, spittle coating the mouthpiece like fresh dew in the early morning hours as Military personnel standing in front of his desk frantically waved their arms for him to stop antagonizing the younger Bin Laden.

Osama's son wasn't privy to Tupac's fiery background; therefore, he didn't expect such a livid threat from a western politician.

"What kind of new President are you speaking with such vulgar words during a serious matter like this?"

Hamza demanded through the phone.

Tupac continued arguing with the younger Bin Laden inexperienced at conducting a hostage situation until a general motioned for the phone promising Hamza that they will consider his demands and call him back shortly.

The military officials shared a plan they had concocted to stall Hamza long enough for them to send in a rescue team to save number 44.

Tupac used his new powers to make sure that they use the same exact Seal team that got the senior Bin Laden back in 2011 but he was displeased that it would take several weeks to implement the plan.

He was more concerned with saving his friend than remaining the President because now that he sat in the big seat he realized that running the highest office in the land wasn't as fun as one would think it would be. At least not for him, anyway.

Over the course of the next seventeen days, Obama was treated fairly by Hamza's men who succumbed to his wit and charm as he told stories about key moments in his life, which made the time go by more pleasantly.

It was hard adjusting to the one bath every three days they allowed him, but the Pakistani food was delicious although they always served it to him cold.

"Now brothers."

Obama began talking one muggy night after toweling off from a nice, cold bath.

"You all know that us infidels love chicken over in America, Especially us Black infidels."

He continued, causing the seven-man guard squad to break out in laughter at his joke.

"Tomorrow when you all bring my rice and Chicken Tikki in here can you please warm it up a little?"

Obama asked jokingly but wearing a serious facial expression.

The former president was fascinated with the account of the Uruguayan rugby team's plane crash in the Andes mountains back in 1972 and how survivors consumed dead human flesh to survive.

Every time he ingested cold chicken, he envisioned what it must have felt like to eat half-frozen human flesh up in those mountains. Yuck!

During those two weeks, President Shakur made several TV appearances on various news outlets, assuring the American people that he would find Obama soon even if he had to gather up an army of Bloods and Crips and ship them all over to the Middle East.

This apparent joke caused a downward spike in the new president's approval ratings mainly due to the slander he received from several Fox News reporters' segments on his incapability to run the country.

"This same guy that wrote song lyrics about our country not being ready to have a Black president is now our sitting president."

Fox News analyst Bill O'Reilly began complaining to an audience of 4 million viewers on his nightly program.

"That's scary people. Mr. Shakur should not be sitting in the Oval Office. He's liable to set off nukes in Compton just to kill some members of a rival gang."

Tupac shoved the off button on the TV remote so hard that he bent his fingernail doing so.

"This mothafucka gonna make me do something to him!"

He barked out to no one in particular as he sat inside of an over-crowded bunker room in the Pentagon awaiting initiation of the rescue mission dubbed *Operation Seal Team Six 2*.

Section 12:

The Showdown

The U.S. Government wired ten million U.S. dollars into an account that Hamza provided as a down payment toward the half-billion he demanded.

"You see, my brothers, we are stronger than the western infidels!"

The overconfident leader shouted as he watched the transaction finalize right before his eyes as he and his men stood in a large room they called their conference room in his Pakistani compound.

As his men were fantasizing about how they would spend the money that was promised to them flash-bang explosions suddenly erupted all around them as Seal Team Six dispersed grenades into the room from open windows after successfully eliminating the two layers of threats that guarded the main house.

Hamza's men were running for cover as they were cut down by the heavy weaponry used by the Navy Seals who filtered into the room through the unlatched casements.

In the end, the same man that pulled the trigger on Osama Bin Laden also pulled the trigger on his son.

The 9/11 Mastermind's son was hit square in his forehead from three rounds out of Senior Chief Petty officer Robert O'Neill's M4A1 carbine and died instantly.

Unfortunate news was reported after the Seals reached the room that Obama was secured in and forced a firefight with Al-Qaeda shooters guarding the slightly huge area.

In the end, all the threats were eliminated but two Seals were killed, and Barack Obama was severely wounded with nine gunshot wounds to his legs, arms, chest, and the rear portion of his head.

As the Hawaiian-Chicagoan lay in a coma at Walter Reed National Military Medical Center, the current president continued to get used to his new role.

All of his past friends were invited to the White House, from Trigger Treach, members of *The Outlaws*, Jada Pinkett-Smith, Kidada Jones, and members of the rap group Digital Underground, to Mike Tyson, singer Danny Boy, rap duo Nice & Smooth, Spice 1, E-40, actor Omar Epps, as well as a host of other people that crossed 'Pac's path throughout his lifetime.

That Fall, President Shakur's approval rating hit the lowest mark any U.S. President had ever reached in history when he held a rally supporting San Francisco 49'ers quarterback Colin Kaepernick who had begun kneeling during the National Anthem at the beginning of football games, which caused an uproar throughout the country, especially from military personnel and patriate extremists.

"You damn right Colin should keep taking a knee!"

Shakur stared at the faces in the crowd of nine-thousand people who had piled into the arena in Atlanta, to hear their outspoken President who started making rhymes out of his campaign quotes.

"Cause I'm the President and they'd even shoot me."

He finished his sentence by referring to the 1969 murder of the Black Panther's Chairman, Fred Hampton, by Chicago P.D. and The F.B.I.

Section 13

Just one week before the 2016 Presidential Election took place Tupac got the call he had been praying for which was that Obama had risen out of his coma and was fully coherent again and wanted to see him.

"I hope your ass is finished pretending to be the president,"

Barack said as Tupac rushed over to his side, leaving his Secret Service security detail at the doorway.

"Hell, Yea Barack. You can have ya' Oval Office back brother. I don't want it anymore."

'Pac laughed as he grabbed his good friend in a bear hug and held him closely.

Tupac then filled Obama in on everything that happened from the time of his rescue until now.

By-election night Obama was healthy enough to be released from the hospital and was taken home, to the White House, where he watched CNN with Tupac and a few other close friends.

"The doctors said I was shot nine times just like you and 50 Cent."

Obama spoke as he looked across the 40-person dining table at Tupac who was carving a slice of his rib-eye steak.

"Nigga you was grazed eight of those nine times so stop it!"

2pac bellowed out in laughter as Obama continued talking.

"Just wait until I go back to Chicago, or as the youngsters call it: *Chiraq*."

The jovial president said, referencing Chicago rappers' usage of the combination of the words Chicago and Iraq to describe their hometown, comparing it to the violence in the middle-eastern nation.

"I'll have more street cred' than you and Nipsey Hussle put together!"

Obama finished as First Lady Michelle looked at her husband with a 'Like really' visage before telling him to hush.

Obama continued joking about his ordeal and how it was like rapper 50 Cent's shooting, and Tupac's two shootings, but in all actuality, eight of the bullets only singed his skin, albeit they still hurt every time he made movement, as they continued to heal.

"I can't believe that Cheeto-head mothafucka beat Hillary!"

An irate Shakur yelled as he stared at Obama's 82" TV screen.

Michelle and Aaliyah retired to another room for girl talk as their husbands sat in the living room watching CNN.

"I did all that I could to help her."

Obama started talking.

"I guess the country really doesn't want to see a female in the White House."

Section 14:

Bye, Bye DMV

During the next couple of months leading up to the new president's inauguration, The Obamas and Shakur's started packing their belongings, preparing to leave Washington.

The president returned to his adopted hometown of Chicago, while Tupac decided to go back to his ministry work, by launching a nationwide tour, distributing Holy Bibles, canned goods, and other materials to people in poverty-stricken neighborhoods.

Aaliyah didn't easily accept the idea of sleeping out of a luxurious motorcoach rather than buying a nice home somewhere and getting used to being regular folks again, but she reluctantly agreed when her man proposed that she simultaneously tour the same cities that he would do ministry work in and promised her that they would buy a home after their tours were over.

She still loved singing despite not having put out a full studio album since her double-platinum, *It's pronounced Ah-liyah, not Uh-liyah* album was released in 2009, so she became excited about hitting the stage again, doing what she loved to do.

Section 15:

Fresh Juice

"Oh shit, my shit is certified triple platinum!"

JuiceWRLD shouted, as he grabbed his girlfriend's head and kissed her lips with violent excitement, as they sat in the kitchen of his $175,000 tour bus.

The Chiraq rapper's debut album, *Goodbye & Good Riddance* sold over 3 million copies and he just ended a phone call with representatives from Billboard who called to confirm his correct mailing address so they could ship his framed plaque out to him.

Things were going well for the new musician but all the new money entering his bank account made it easier for him to continue abusing the various narcotics that he was addicted to.

As his fame increased he even dabbled in drugs that he had never tried before, which assisted in his continued addiction. His friends and family couldn't wait for the day that he broke free of his dependence because they had faith in Jarad turning out to be the outstanding man that they knew and loved.

By early 2019, JuiceWRLD released his second studio album, Death Race for Love, which debuted at number 1 on the U.S. Billboard charts and solidified his spot in the world of music.

Section 16:

House on the lake

While the melodic rapper and his team were putting the final touches on the initial tour for his second album, Tupac and his queen were wrapping up their respective tours.

Initially intending to spend a year out on the road, the cozy couple extended that time to two years, primarily because Aaliyah missed her fans and relished reuniting with them.

She even ran into new fans, that she hadn't met before, from Kim Kardashian-West, Boston Celtic's center-forward Robert Williams III, to actress Zendaya, and rappers Drake and J. Cole.

"Bae, I just found our new house. It's out in Marin county where me and momma used to live."

Tupac spoke as he checked out the mansion's description on a phone app called *Zillow* while he and Aaliyah lay in the queen-sized bed located in the rear of their motorhome as it rumbled up Interstate 95.

The former thug rapper spent the last eighteen months visiting several U.S. cities, passing out Bibles and other free items to the passerby, as he and his staff stood at tables in the poorest neighborhoods in those cities.

Tupac's Secret Service security detail wasn't too particularly fond of the locations he chose to make these distributions, but they all understood that Tupac was a man of the people, therefore he would always go where the people were, whether it be the most dangerous area in South Central, Los Angeles to the borough with the highest crime rate in New York City.

Scores of people who would have never stepped foot inside of a church were able to receive a Holy Bible because Tupac brought the church to their environment.

There were a few areas where he came across resistance when he attempted to pass out Bibles though.

Primarily in front of nightclubs and other high-traffic venues which never went well with the owners and bouncers.

One night while setting up four tables filled with Bibles, canned goods, and boxes of tabletop oscillating fans in front of the upscale club *Liv* in Miami Beach, club security came out to confront Tupac about interfering with their clubgoers but were quickly turned around by Shakur's Secret Service protection.

The long line of people waiting to enter the establishment was subjected to Tupac's mobile speakers playing T.D. Jakes and Joel Osteen's sermons, causing some of the sinners to turn and leave due to feelings of conviction of wrongdoing.

"I don't want to go back to California."

Aaliyah said puzzling Tupac who thought his wife loved Cali'.

"There are too many fake people out there and I'd rather stay in the east and go back to New York."

"Baby, it's west side til' I die. Come on now." 'Pac pleaded with his spouse.

They spent the next half hour going back and forth about where they should call home when Tupac decided to compromise with her by agreeing to set up their main residence in the east and spend their summers out on the west coast.

Aaliyah, then threw her man another curve ball revealing that she wanted them to relocate to upstate N.Y., instead of their birthplace. When she mentioned that she wanted to move to New York Tupac automatically assumed she meant Manhattan or somewhere closer to the five boroughs.

Like really. Where else would a New Yorker want to live, if not inside of, or in close proximity to the greatest city in the entire world?

The rest of New York State is just nothingness when compared to NYC.

"Bae, where the fuck is a Skaneateles?"

Tupac whined after Aaliyah named the town she wanted to make home.

She explained that, back in D.C. Hillary told her about Skaneateles and that it was a beautiful little village in upstate NY that her family vacationed in back at the turn of the Millennium and was also discovered by the likes of Yankees great, Derek Jeter and a few of the Baldwin brothers who all made the two-stoplight burg their homes, at one point in time.

After consulting with a local real estate agent, The Shakurs narrowed their house search down to three properties, settling on a 5.7-million-dollar palace on the lake that was only four mansions down from the home that the Clintons stayed in almost two decades prior.

When the local media got wind of who was moving into the area it was as if the circus had come to town.

Fans of both 2pac and Aaliyah made the trek from the neighboring city of Syracuse, which was the largest town in the region of Central New York, and less than 30 minutes away.

The former U.S. President was glad that his new house had an 8-foot wrought-iron gate surrounding the property because after the Syracuse faithful began camping out on the boundaries of his land just to get a glimpse of the thug-turned-Commander-in-Chief and his extraordinary wife, fellow fans from other upstate N.Y. cities like Albany, Rochester, Binghamton, and even as distant as Buffalo started pulling up and giving Tupac's Secret Service detail headaches as they scrambled to provide full protection for the controversial-yet-beloved humanitarian.

The Shakurs were the talk of the town but managed to piss some Syracusans off one muggy Saturday after Aaliyah expressed a desire to go shopping, which prompted Tupac to have the Secret Service contact the Syracuse Police Department's Chief, Kenton Buckner who authorized the closing of Destiny USA Mall, the eighth largest mall in America so the couple could shop in private.

As the Shakurs' motorcade rolled through the mid-size city, one of the Secret Service agents who happened to be a native of the nearby town of Utica, New York gave the Shakur's a tour.

"This is the city's southside. This is where most of the African American population resides in this town."

The light-skinned agent said as the motorcade of black Chevy Tahoes and Suburbans drove down South Salina street.

The smooth-talking agent pointed out the Carrier Dome on the Syracuse University campus, and the neighboring Pioneer Homes housing projects, which were the first low-income housing complex built in America.

As the caravan made its way onto South Geddes street the talkative political policeman asked Tupac to guess what side of town they were on and after the Ministry leader shrugged his shoulders in an 'I don't know' gesture, agent Howard informed him that they were on the west side of town, which elicited Tupac to press the button that opened the SUV's rear sunroof, allowing him to pop his head out of the top of the truck and yell "Westside!!!", as Puerto Rican and black onlookers recognized their ex-president, one of the biggest rappers in history.

They started shouting "Tu-Pac!" repeatedly as The Secret Service attempted to pull 'Pac back down into the safety of the bulletproof Suburban.

Section 17:

Powers

After 120 days in upstate N.Y., the Shakurs were settling in and enjoying their new chapter in life, but in early December of that year, Almighty God summoned Tupac back to Heaven, marking the final chapter of his life on the present earth.

"Bae, wake up!"

An exhilarated Aaliyah spoke loudly into 'Pac's right ear as they lay in their California King-sized bed.

"Wake your ass up boy it's time."

She finished, pouring the half-drank bottle of Aquafina on the nightstand, in his face as he lay snoring loudly.

'Damn 'Liyah what the fuck bae!"

A half-woke Tupac grumbled as his wife explained to him that Almighty God is about to transport them back to Heaven to grant him his powers, which will allow him to complete his earthly mission.

Before a groggy Shakur could fully comprehend what the love of his life had just said, he and she were instantly teleported from their Skaneateles mansion's master bedroom to the same room that they were in on their last visit to Paradise.

The room was dimly lit, and the angel Nathaniel emerged from the shadows of a corner of the large area.

"Long time no see mate."

He said shaking Tupac's hand before hugging Aaliyah, letting her know that the other angels miss her deeply and can't wait for her mission to be concluded so she could return to Heaven for good.

An over-anxious 'Pac interrupted the sentimental moment by asking a question concerning his receiving special powers, unable to contain himself.

"So, is this gonna be like some Luke Skywalker and Yoda shit in that old Star Wars movie where you train me to get these powers?"

Nathaniel exploded in laughter as he snapped the fingers on his left hand which caused the room to suddenly illuminate.

"You humans watch too many movies!"

He said motioning for them to sit down in the same chairs they used during their last visit.

The good-natured angel then explained to Tupac that he already has the powers in him which is God's Holy Spirit and that they only needed to be activated for him to begin using them.

"So, let's get started," Nathaniel said as a third chair miraculously appeared out of thin air in front of the lovebirds.

After sitting down, he made a 'come closer' gesture with his hands, prompting Tupac and Aaliyah to lean forward as the angel grabbed one of each of their hands forming a prayer circle.

Bowing his head, Nathaniel began praying and thanking Lord God for everything He does for his fellow angels, the human race and the earthly animals, and other forms of life, and how grateful everyone is to have a merciful God like Him.

"And by the power vested in me, I hereby grant those same powers to the human named Tupac Shakur."

The angel man said, wrapping up his prayer.

Just like Nathaniel told him during his first encounter with him, the data that Tupac needed to use his powers was instantly downloaded into his brain and he shot up from his chair more excited than the character he played in the movie *Juice* when Raheem handed over the chrome .38 revolver to him in the park.

As Tupac extended both hands out to hug his angel friend in an act of gratitude, he fell forward onto his bed as Aaliyah, and he instantly reappeared back in their bedroom.

After a moment of silence, he looked at his wife and started grinning before blood walk dancing around the room as he made his way towards her, picking her up and tickling her.

"Being the President wasn't shit compared to what I can do now."

He laughed, recalling all of the magical stuff that Nathaniel performed during their first meeting.

Aaliyah warned him about the dangers of power abuse which she didn't have to because The Holy Spirit already communicated to his human spirit that his powers wouldn't work unless being used for the sole purpose of why he was given them, which was to encounter the rap artist named *JuiceWRLD* and give him the same instructions that the angel Nathaniel had given him years ago.

A determined Tupac awakened the following morning thrilled about possessing particular powers, in spite of the fact that he couldn't use them at his leisure.

"I gotta track that kid JuiceWRLD down ASAP."

He thought to himself as he rose to get out of bed, noticing his sexy wife still asleep, laying on her stomach, wearing tight silk pajamas which turned him on.

After gently pulling the bottom half of her sleepwear down past the rear portions of her thighs, a horny Tupac began planting pas-

133

sionate kisses on her buttocks before moving all of the ways down to her freshly pedicured feet, smearing saliva stains all over them with his serpently tongue.

Aaliyah became aroused and popped her eyes open in delight, grabbing her mate's head and shoving it towards her crotch before he slammed on his neck's brakes, noticing the pad sticking out of her nether region.

"Damn babe I ain't no damn vampire, what the fuck?"

2pac blurted out, playfully annoyed.

"Well, you shouldn't be starting stuff."

Aaliyah giggled as she grabbed her phone to call their house-keeper to inform her of what she wanted for breakfast.

'Pac hopped in the shower and after getting dressed in a Versace tracksuit, grabbed his iPhone 11 to log in to *Instagram* and send *JuiceWRLD* a direct message.

After patiently waiting four hours for a reply DM from Jarad, 2pac decided to utilize the Secret Service, who were able to hack into the star rapper's phone records to obtain his cell phone number.

As soon as the man on a mission received it he immediately dialed Juice's number. Most celebrities don't answer strange numbers, but Jarad Higgins was stricken with Obsessive-Compulsive disorder when it came to answering his phone. It didn't matter if the caller had an area code from South Dakota, Juice was going to accept the call.

This helped Tupac out because when he placed his call, Jarad answered his new iPhone 11 Pro Max instantly.

"Who is this?" He asked casually as he lounged in his hotel room at the Ritz-Carlton in Los Angeles.

"Hey JuiceWRLD, this is Tupac and- "

A mellow-feeling Jarad, floating high off of Opioids, perceived the caller as a prankster.

"Man, get the fuck outta here! You ain't no damn Tupac, bitch!"

He shouted into his phone's mouthpiece before ending the call forcefully with his right index finger.

Minutes later the intoxicated artist called his girlfriend Ally and told her about the prank call, but he didn't receive the loyalty he thought she was going to give him.

Instead of agreeing with him that he did the right thing by terminating the call, Ally asked the question: "What if that was Tupac?"

Which prompted the foggy-minded rapper to recall the brief call and play it back in his mind.

"Damn, that kind of did sound like 2pac."

He thought to himself, remembering watching news footage of President Shakur when he was assuring the American people that he would get Obama back home safely a few years ago.

"Damn, that was 'Pac!"

JuiceWRLD broke out of his haziness, turning the TV volume down, before dialing Tupac's number.

Shakur answered his phone as soon as it rang and Jarad apologized to him, apprising the former president that he thought it was a prank call.

Tupac laughed and informed the hitmaker that he had important things to discuss with him and needed to see him, in person, as soon as possible.

"Naw, forget that! Do you know that my name is *JuiceWRLD* because of yo' movie?"

He excitedly informed 'Pac, referring to 2pac's part in *Juice*, which he named himself after, adding the *WRLD* on the end to emphasize that he had the Juice, and the world was his for the taking.

This sentimentality moved 2pac's heart and he distractedly spent the next twenty minutes sharing stories about what transpired on the set of the movie making Jarad love his favorite movie of all time even more.

"Where are you right now Juice? I need to see you in person."

Shakur asked, gliding back on track.

"I'm out here in yo' state 'Pac. Westsiiiiide!!!"

Jarad replied, indicating that he was in California.

"But me and my team'll be leaving here around 5:30 p.m. on a PJ, headed home to Chicago."

Tupac glanced at his phone's clock and saw that Jarad would depart Los Angeles within three hours, west coast time, which was three hours behind New York's time zone, making it impossible to link up with him by hopping on a plane so 'Pac made the resolution to use his special powers for the first time to contact the target of his mission.

"You can meet me in Chicago tomorrow if that's what you want to do,"

Jarad said, continuing the conversation as he walked over to the window of his suite, looking down at the street's activity from 45 stories up.

After several seconds of silence, Juice spoke into his phone's mouthpiece asking Tupac if he was still on the line.

"No, Juice I'm right here brother."

'Pac spoke, as he sat on the edge of Jarad's hotel room's bed.

"What the fuck!!!"

JuiceWRLD turned around, hopping two feet in the air, staring at Tupac with an expression of astonishment.

"Bro, I love you but how did you get into my room?"

"By the power of Jesus Christ,"

2pac answered before explaining to the 21-year-old why he had to make contact with him, and what God had made him undergo, to prepare him for the present moment.

"Wait a minute, wait a minute 'Pac." A skeptical Jarad said, interrupting his dialogue.

"You want me to believe that Jesus Christ gave you superpowers, and now you're a fuckin Avenger like Thor or Captain America?"

Jarad asked, looking at his idol in a different light.

Soon after Tupac replied, "Of course."

Jarad was instantly teleported from his plush hotel room to an empty movie theater, the same way the angel Nathaniel did with Tupac years earlier.

JuiceWRLD, seated in the front row of the humongous room, looked at the all-white screen before turning around to view what was behind him.

In the very last row of seats, center screen sat a smiling Tupac who said

"If you're too close to the screen you can always come back here and sit with me pot'nah."

Jarad slowly rose from his front-row chair with a quizzical look on his face as he made the journey to the rear of the cinema, dropping his body down next to 'Pac's.

"Alright ', Pac, I don't know what the fuck is going on, but I believe you, bro' cuz I know goddamn well I ain't trippin' off some bad Perc's I took earlier 'cause I get the real shit straight from an RN."

Jarad finished, revealing that his drug connection is an actual nurse, and not some strange, street dealer.

Before Jarad could begin asking questions the silver screen began playing footage of him and his entourage, boarding a private jet in Los Angeles, bound for Mid-way airport in Chicago, in the future, which would be today, and tomorrow morning.

During the flight, Jarad pours water on one of his sleeping co-horts, as part of a practical joke, then finally nestled into his seat for the landing.

After an attempt to deplane the aircraft, Jarad and his team were detained in handcuffs by F.B.I. agents, and Chicago P.D. for suspicion of drugs onboard a plane, after the pilot alerted authorities upon boarding back in L.A.

Fearing drug charges due to the 70 pounds of marijuana, and bottles of codeine and Percocet pills stuffed in his suitcases, Jarad panicked and swallowed a handful of them that were sitting in his pocket, causing him to begin convulsing and later die at an Illinois hospital.

The footage continued rolling on the cinema's big screen, showing the aftermath of Jarad's soon death, with friends, fans, and family all mourning their great loss.

"I don't wanna see no more, 'Pac!!!"

An emotional Higgins shouted out as he broke out in tears, the weight of his imminent demise causing the opioid high to quickly fade away.

Suddenly the footage stopped, and as the huge screen went dark blank, the theater's lights slowly came on.

Tupac cocked his head to the right to look at the weeping young man and spoke.

"Yea, Juice that's how yo' life is about to play out if you don't obey the O.G."

Wiping his eyes dry with the ends of his Balenciaga tee, Jarad looked at Tupac confused, and asked him what did his death have to do with an old gangster from the streets, making reference to the urban moniker, 'O.G.' which stood for *Original Gangsta,* used by younger guys in the streets, when addressing, or communicating with someone older, who has been involved in more criminal activity based on their active years.

"No, nigga." Tupac started laughing.

"I'm talking about Almighty God. I call him The O.G. because He's the One God, the Only God, and the Original God."

JuiceWRLD started laughing as he understood but his heart was still sunken from the death news he had just received.

"Bro' I don't wanna die man. I'm just 21 and me and my girl ain't even have a baby yet."

Juice continued talking.

"And I don't know if you follow me on social media, but you see this tatt'?"

Jarad held out his left arm and pointed at a tattoo reading the numbers '999'.

"I'm a positive dude bro'. I took the numbers 666 from the Bible and flipped them around to 999, which means taking negative shit that happened to you and turning it into something positive."

Tupac was surprised at this revelation because Jarad didn't come across as someone who was spiritual, although he didn't appear to be some young soul lost in the streets either.

"So, what does the O.G. want me to do so He don't let me die tomorrow?"

"I'm glad you asked young man."

'Pac replied as he started rising from the stiff-cushioned movie theater seat, and in a split second his right arm was extended towards the young rapper, with a Holy Bible at the end of it as they stood on the same tree-lined dirt road that Nathaniel used.

"Damn this shit is like a video game or switching scenes in a movie."

Jarad remarked as he looked around at the spooky-looking woodland.

"First, The O.G. wants you to stop doing drugs,"

Shakur informed him, making his knees wobble.

Telling this extreme substance abuser to cease his daily narcotics intake was tantamount to telling a White Nationalist, who suffered from paranoia due to the *Great Replacement Theory,* to allow his only daughter to marry a Black man.

It would be hard as fuck to do but Jarad's existence was in jeopardy, and he wanted to remain alive more than he wanted to get lit off of weed, lean, and Perc's.

"Bro' tell the O.G. I quit right now!"

Juice blurted out even though he still desired to abuse drugs.

"He also wants you to begin speaking out about the dangers of doing drugs, so your story can influence others to follow your path of sobriety."

Tupac continued as he kneeled to lay in the grass on the road's edge.

"You do know that I have the ability to read your thoughts, right?"

Shakur revealed as Jarad remained standing on the dirt road, his cool grey Jordan 11s coated in dust.

"Nooo, I'm keeping it a hundred with you 'Pac!"

Higgins spoke loudly, staring down at Tupac with sincerity in his teary eyes.

'Pac assured him that he knew that and was fully convinced that he was about to turn his life around, which comforted the young rapper, because that meant that God was going to give him a second chance at life, by not allowing him to perish from the overdose he would have suffered tomorrow.

As Tupac bent his elbows and knees to lift himself off of the ground, a loud animal howl startled Jarad who whipped his head around as fast as he could, because the sound came from behind him, and after assessing the noise as a non-threat he turned back around to glance at 'Pac but he wasn't there, although the grass that he was just lying in was slowly bending back into an upright shape.

After moving his eyeballs around frantically for a few seconds, eyeing the creepy wood-lined road, he was teleported back into his hotel room, which made him breathe a sigh of relief.

Section 18:

Changes

The man of his word immediately grabbed his iPhone off the night-stand and tweeted,

To all of my fans and drug users across the world, please follow my lead by stopping using and abusing drugs!

En route to Los Angeles International airport, some of his entourage who saw the tweet questioned him about it, wondering if it was just a clout chasing move.

Jarad also received a call from his girlfriend, Ally, who praised him for the tweet and assured him that she loved him and couldn't wait to start a family with him.

Before reaching the airport, Jarad told the driver to pull over near the dumpsters in the parking lot of a huge restaurant. He hopped out and went to the rear of the Sprinter van and commenced slinging several of his suitcases into the row of trash containers lining the wall of the building, shocking his traveling group.

"Yo' what the fuck is wrong with Juice?"

One friend asked another as they witnessed the rapper throwing away thousands of dollars worth of marijuana and prescription pills.

As they arrived at the airport and boarded the luxurious jet, the nosey pilot called authorities about suspicion of drugs on board his plane because of an incident, a month earlier, where he piloted Jarad and his group to Atlanta and received verbal abuse from them because he accused the group of smoking weed in the plane's lavatory despite having any evidence to have them arrested.

Upon landing at Chicago's Mid-way International airport, The plane's passengers were all detained by law enforcement, but no drugs or weapons were discovered aboard, which forced Chicago P.D. to release everyone.

One of Jarad's zealous friends wound up getting arrested for simple battery after knocking the pilot out cold with one uppercut, as he exited the area.

"Snitches get stitches!"

The loyal friend shouted at the unconscious airman, as he stepped over his body towards the policemen.

Just three months after having his life spared by God, a rejuvenated Jarad Higgins sat in his condo's living room with his girlfriend, watching a segment on CNN about an outbreak of a new pathogen called *Coronavirus-19* when a newsbreak interrupted that program.

Long-time commentator, Don Lemon appeared on-screen and announced that he had sad news.

"Folks, I'm sorry to report this but the 45th president of the United States and his wife, Grammy Award-winning singer/actress Aaliyah were just hospitalized a few hours ago.

We are still gathering details so we can make an accurate report to you all, but doctors have confirmed that they both have passed away due to severe respiratory infections possibly from this new virus."

The somber newsman explained as he stared into the studio cameras revealing his heartbreak.

Jarad Higgins wept like a baby, primarily because he had just encountered 2pac in December, and now he was gone in March.

The saved rapper fought the urge to post details of his time with 'Pac because it was a supernatural visit so he couldn't reveal it to someone without them thinking he was crazy, therefore he kept it to himself.

JuiceWRLD kept his promise and never touched another Percocet, or any other narcotic from the day he met Tupac, even launching a nonprofit organization promoting the dangers of using drugs which reached millions of people who adored JuiceWRLD's music and followed his lead.

Parting shots

Yo, this shit was fire right?!?!

Word to me I got more entertainment on the way!

The rapper *Drake* released a song back in 2012 titled, *'The Motto'* where he rapped about humans only living once but that isn't true because Tupac and Aaliyah are still alive, only in a different realm.

The story of their continuance, as well as many others, will be explored in part two of this masterpiece. Keep watching, Yo!

About Author

G.K. David II is a rapper, author, and founder of a non-profit organization (God's Government, Inc.).

The God-made-man hails from Syracuse, N.Y., and graduated from National Tractor Trailer School in 2015. After driving trucks for 4 years, he was involved in a near-fatal accident in upstate New York.

With extra time on his hands as he healed from his injury, he began brainstorming ideas about writing a book and released a children's book on Amazon in 2021.

The creative genius decided to launch his own publishing company afterward and write his first novel, *The Continuance*.

www.ingramcontent.com/pod-product-compliance
Lightning Source LLC
Chambersburg PA
CBHW070047260626
47159CB00005B/2141